THE WHALEMASTER

FOR MY WONDERFUL WIFE AND SON,
AND MY GRANDFATHER, M. MACHADO.

The WHALE master

MICHAEL MONIZ

SIMPLY READ BOOKS

WHALING GROUNDS
HUNTING THE SPERM WHALE

EUROPE

United Kingdom

AFRICA

PORTUGAL

AZORES

NORTH AMERICA

BERMUDA

AZORES
THE 9 ISLANDS

Corvo

Flores

Graciosa

Terceira

São Jorge

Faial

Pico

São Miguel

Santa Maria

WHERE THE HAWKS SOAR

B etween the old world and the new lie the nine islands. Discovered and settled by the Portuguese in the early 1400s, they float like an oasis of green amidst a vast and rolling sea. The early explorers named the archipelago the Azores for the many hawks they found flying over the coastal cliffs.

The nine islands are distinct from one another, with varying landscapes and climate. Volcanic in origin, they are famous for their natural wonders and beauty. Throughout history the great ships of trade and war have sought sanctuary there, ferrying soldiers and gold between continents.

LETTER TO ABRAHAM STRINGER

FROM
CAPTAIN NATHANIEL STRINGER

OF THE *SURE PROFIT* OUT OF BEDFORD, NEW ENGLAND

AUGUST 22, 1764

Dear Abraham,

I hope this letter finds you, and finds you well. For myself, things are growing increasingly desperate.

Forgive me for not finding occasion to write you sooner. My moods have grown black—I scarcely sleep, and am finding it increasingly difficult to eat as my digestion suffers on ship. I am worried, dear brother.

The pods are nowhere in sight, the barrels near empty. We have come by a few ships that have fared pretty well, and are headed for home. I don't understand it. I feel cursed. To be frank, dear brother, my fortune is in peril. God help me.

Though there is still hope: the Azores lie west of us, untouched, teeming with the oil-filled giants that swim about their shores.

I doubt you have heard much of anything about them, as they are in a remote and secretive place if ever there was one. My stomach turns at the idea of making such a voyage. I had hoped to secure my fortune closer to home. Many myths and stories abound about these Azores. Some say the legendary city of Atlantis dwells beneath them, others that whole kingdoms have been swallowed up many times over as the islands change and move throughout time. But the most lingering tales are of what lives in the deep, for many swear the nine are home to monsters and giants, sleeping in wait for us, beneath volcanic shores.

It is nonsense, I know, but the tales fill me with hope. Hope for oil, hope for fortune.

Please look in on my wife, Martha. I so do miss her terribly. We owe you much, dear brother, I know. Pray for me, brother, as I pray for you. I grow tired; these damnable worries are more than I can bear.

Nathaniel

"But all the gods pitied him except Poseidon;
he remained relentlessly angry with godlike Odysseus,
until his return to his own country."

— HOMER, *THE ODYSSEY*

year of our lord

1765

THE BLACK

I t is dark at these depths, too dark for eyes to see. So he clicks and creaks, calling out in the blackness. A pulsing noise that ripples through the liquid night. The vibrations bounce back, reverberating inside his head, forming images of everything that surrounds him.

He clamps down on his meal, the toothy tentacles of his prey writhing between his curved teeth. He savors the chewy sensation. He ignores the pain as the tentacles rake across his cheeks, making him bleed. In its death throes the tentacled thing fouls the water with a jet of black ink. He shakes his massive head and swims through the oily black.

He likes feeding down here in the darkness. It won't be long before his meal—beak, toothy arms and all—is digested and his hunger quelled.

Nothing escapes him down here. This is his home, his last feeding ground.

The pods are mostly gone now, scattered, hiding anywhere they can. But not him; he won't leave. He will make them suffer for what they have done, the boats with their little men.

They're relentless little monsters, filling the water with his blood, driving the sharp iron through him. He kills and kills, but still they come.

Their sharp weapons stay with him, dragging along in his wounds. Some have fallen out, but many remain.

The men came from the bits of land in the middle of his sea. The little boats spew out from those islands, turning the water into a killing ground. His kin slaughtered and butchered.

How long before he'll be the very last? He clicks out to the blackness, to the endless silence.

He lies in wait, resting and waiting for the blood and fire to return.

The blackness soothes and comforts him; small creatures glow in the black, beckoning with their ghostly light. He feels ancient, tired and broken. There is peace here in the dark, rest for his festering wounds.

As he floats, a fire flickers overhead, crimson and gold light dancing above him, disturbing the calm. Thunderous sounds echo. The men are back with their floating tubs.

He arches his back, feeling it spasm. One long wound has refused to heal; it stings with a salty pain. They will pay in blood, the ocean stained red with it.

With a mighty effort he twists his bulky body and swims upwards, towards the booming ships.

RUNNING UP THE RED FLAG

A ship is a pretty thing: its complex of ropes, pulleys and timber, its sails billowing—ghostly and beautiful over the water.

They were closing in on the ship. Soon the screaming would start and dragon fire would be licking at those pretty white sails.

Captain Dougan, also known as the 'Dragon' to those who feared him, grinned broadly. Another ship would be his and all its treasures surrendered.

He wore a splendid red uniform with shining black boots. Sashes stuffed with pistols and daggers crisscrossed his broad chest. His eyes were ice blue. His hair and beard both a curling, golden blonde. He was a tall and fierce figure, dashing and regal.

The Spanish had given him the name 'Dragon' after a particularly lucrative pillaging of one of their treasure ships. The Spaniards had a hard time pronouncing his name, so 'Dougan' became 'Dragon', a title better suited to his nature.

He carried a long-sword with an ornate pummel in the shape of a serpent that twisted and wrapped itself around the metal handle. His face, tanned bronze, was without blemish or wrinkle. A single gold tooth gleamed out from a menacing grin.

"Lower those colors! Raise the dragon!" Dougan roared.

It was a common trick. To fool a merchant vessel with its own country's flag, the old flag of England. His own emblem was very fitting, a black dragon in a field of red—a fearsome sight for any ship on these waters.

"Fire one of the cannons. Careful not to hit them, Mr. Scrab," the captain boomed. "A close shave will do!"

"Aye, Captain!" said the old pirate quartermaster.

Scrab was a gruesome figure. He had only one leg and hobbled around on a wooden stump. His ancient face was lined with old scars and deep wrinkles, like a discarded piece of torn leather. He wore a large, floppy hat and carried a heavy saber. His black clothes were covered in stains. Inside his dozen pockets he carried an untold number of knives and daggers. Scrab was just as awful as he looked. He was unmatched, except perhaps by the captain himself, in the arts of cruelty. In all the seas, the captain's black soul was undoubtedly the blackest.

The *Red Gull* shuddered with each roar of the cannon. There was no other ship like her; a twenty-six-gun frigate with a reinforced hull tinted a deep crimson. It was a deadly man-o'-war, with a crew of over two hundred cutthroats and murderers to man her.

The merchant ship was a heavy, slow thing, with only sixteen useless cannons. The crew of twenty could barely manage to fire three of the puny guns at once. The balls rattled harmlessly against the reinforced hull of the pirate ship, bouncing off and into the sea.

"Prepare the men, Mr. Scrab," said the captain, suppressing a tired yawn.

"Get yourselves together, lads! We board them soon," Scrab yelled.

The filthy crew huddled around him. Their grappling hooks, pistols and axes at the ready. As the men hooted and yelped, the opposing crew scrambled with fear, trembling behind their muskets.

The merchant ship crackled, dainty plumes of white smoke obscuring its riggings. A cannonball rumbled across the pirate deck, crushing one of the crew as it passed.

"They dare!" croaked Scrab. "Let fly, men!"

Grenadoes spun in the air, whizzing and sparkling before exploding on the merchant vessel. The panic-stricken crew on the merchant ship began to scream as they crouched low for cover.

Dougan coolly watched a helmsman stagger backwards, his chest blown out. The sailor at the wheel next to him fell from a musket ball, and the merchant ship veered to starboard.

Grappling hooks flew out from the *Red Gull*, hitching and pulling the hapless ship alongside.

A white flag waved in the air. Not soon enough for the Dragon.

Dougan was the first over the side and was welcomed by the startled face of a young midshipman as he thudded onto the merchant deck. The man crumpled beneath the Dragon's sword. The Dragon continued into the mess of men, his blade gleaming as it hacked down the helpless crew.

Scrab was cackling madly, the head of the merchant ship's captain cradled in his arm.

Big Billy, every inch of him covered in tattoos, gave a threatening roar. His painted face and torso were splattered red, his axe dripping with gore.

The pirates ignored the pleas for mercy as they ran wild, the deck slippery beneath their boots. Now in a desperate frenzy, the merchant crew began throwing themselves headlong overboard.

The Dragon relished the moment, closing his eyes and inhaling the acrid scent of iron and blood. Dougan was born for this life. He was no ordinary man after all. He was the captain, the Dragon, and the single greatest scourge of all the Atlantic.

The merchant vessel's sails glowed an eerie orange in the smoke. The flames crawled up the masts.

"Damn!" Dougan cursed. He would have to be quick. It would not be long now before the ship burned completely, sinking into the deep.

"Take what you can and kill the rest of them! This ship will turn to kindling in this breeze," Dougan shouted.

"Candles!" spat Scrab. "The ship's full of candles, silks and finery, Captain."

Dougan groaned. Merchant ships carried many goods and the like for the new world. The candles and items of fashion held a high price, and were much sought after. Now they would only help the ship burn up all the faster.

The pirates leapt off, leaving their dead victims behind them. They pushed away the burning ship with long pikes, a heavy black smoke rising from it, the smell of smoldering flesh carried in the air above it.

"A shame," said the ship's sailing master, Talbot Croon. Talbot was a fat, waddling figure with a tall, feathered hat and red beard. He was touchy about his missing ear, and his wide red face gave him a fevered, angry appearance. He had been pressed into service from a captured ship not long ago, but even still, he was well liked by the men and Dougan resented him for it.

"Ha! There will be more ships. Don't you concern yourself," Dougan growled.

"We opened up too soon on 'em," grumbled Talbot.

"Not fast enough!" snarled Scrab.

"Don't be so squeamish, Croon. When the flag goes up, I expect immediate surrender. After all, we have a reputation to maintain." Dougan chuckled.

"Reputation? There's no one left on that blasted ship! What stories be coming out of that mess, Captain?"

"Exactly. No one fires on my ship and lives to tell the tale. This is all part of the game; breathe it in, Talbot. This is what glory smells like."

Talbot looked back and forth at Scrab and Dougan, shaking his head.

Dougan gave his sailing master a dark look; why he tolerated the weak fool was beyond him. He'd never even seen the man slit a throat.

"Captain, look there!" exclaimed Scrab, thrusting a blackened finger at the flaming ship.

A woman was visible now, calling to the pirate crew. She had long, black hair and wore a white dress, which was blowing before the flames. A boy stood clinging to her, a child no more than ten or so. He was frozen in fear, his face streaked with soot and tears.

"The woman must have been hiding below," Talbot muttered.

The captain's face flushed. "Stupid," he sighed, shaking his head.

"Should I send over a few of the men, Captain?" Talbot asked, twisting his thick beard. "Save the lass and her whelp?"

Dougan winced, considering the matter. "Bah!" he blustered. "That ship will crash in on itself soon enough. No sense in risking any of the men."

Scrab grunted and gave the captain a reassuring nod. "Best keep the woman away. Bad luck aboard ship and all."

"But they could be worth something. Ransom maybe?" Talbot blurted.

Dougan scowled. "Look at them. They're poor wretches, worthless. Probably bartered everything they had for passage on that ship. You're a fool, Talbot, a damn fool."

Talbot lowered his gaze, the captain's eyes burrowing in on him.

The woman was pleading in a shrill voice from her ruined ship. "Save him," she shouted, motioning to her petrified son.

The crew of the *Red Gull* jeered at the desperate woman.

The pirates leaned casually against the railing, waiting for the ship to sink and put the two survivors out of their misery.

"Will that damn ship ever go down?" Dougan growled.

"Won't be long now, Captain," said Scrab.

The crew waved mockingly, the woman clasping hands with the child before jumping overboard. They hit the water hard, waves crashing over them, threatening to swallow them whole.

Two heads emerged from the rolling water. Dougan caught sight of their frightened faces just as the flaming ship keeled over. There came a loud crack—the jumble of wood and sails folding over, sinking into the sea.

They were gone.

"Pity," Talbot whispered.

There was nothing left of the ship on the choppy water, just the greasy black cloud of its extinguished fire, slowly trailing and evaporating over the pirate vessel.

"Aye," muttered Scrab. "Least it was quick!"

There was silence, the men looking out at the grey foaming sea as the surface cleared. The bloody work was done.

The captain scratched his beard, shivered slightly from the cool breeze and turned towards the upper ship.

He reeled at a strange and sudden noise, a loud clicking sound growing through the ship.

He drew his sword instinctively and struggled to keep his balance—the vessel was shaking, sending men tumbling down around him.

Dougan's first thought was that they were caught in the pull of the sinking merchant ship, but that ship was long gone, and too far below. He could feel a terrible pressure, something pushing against his ship's hull.

Scrab's wooden leg screeched along the wet deck as he struggled to keep himself up.

A long creaking vibrated up the timbers. It sounded as though the *Red Gull* were breaking apart, the wood splintering along the ship's bottom.

"Look!" Talbot gasped, pointing to a huge shadow rippling in the water off the port side. The ominous shadow dove, vanished and quickly appeared again off the stern. The vessel rocked violently from side to side with its swell, the captain yelling to hold fast.

Suddenly, a mass of wrinkled grey flesh erupted on the surface, covered in salty white, crisscrossing scars. Ropes flowed out from the beast, trailing from its back like long, black eels. A horrible, pale gash peeled along the creature's side, visible from one end of the monster's crested form to the other. The wound looked like it had festered, neither bleeding nor healing, and had been bleached white. This was a leviathan, a beast belched up from hell.

"It's Jonah's whale! God's monster sent to swallow us whole," yelled old Lob. He was even older than Scrab with huge, chewed-up ears and a hollow socket where his right eye should be.

"Brace yourselves, lads!" Scrab yelled.

The beast crested close, dwarfing Dougan's ship. It circled, the loose flesh rippling with the waves. Its blowhole spluttered and sprayed jets of water at an odd angle.

The creature's clicking grew louder, the deck rolling wildly with the swelling sea. The men gripped the gunwales with white knuckles, their stomachs lurching with fear.

"Prepare to fire!" yelled Dougan, swinging angrily with his sword. "Blow that thing out of the water before it smashes us to kindling!"

Muskets blazed and cannons boomed. The creature slid off the ship and dove away deftly, enveloped in the sea.

The creature's shadow bobbed off the bow, its gargantuan head slowly rising—square, with swollen eyes. It seemed to stare for a moment, peering at the men with its reflective gaze.

The head rolled away fluidly, waves battering the ship's sides.

The creature bent its hulking hump, the ticking quickening in its throat, like something grinding beneath the sea. Old Lob covered his gnarled ears and gnashed his few remaining teeth.

The beast swerved, slamming its head against the hull, the sound of rushing water below deck as the creature ripped away from the ship.

Its tail pointed straight, water churning around it as it went down into the black.

"What was that?" gasped Talbot, picking himself up.

"A whale, just a whale; deformed and monstrous, but a whale all the same. The whalers have been at it, wounding it some," said Dougan. "What damage to the hull, Mr. Scrab?"

The old pirate was peering over the railing, the men clustered all around him. "We're taking on water, that much is for sure. Too much water, Captain."

"How bad?"

Scrab shrugged. "We'll man the pumps and stay afloat a while, Captain, but my guess is we'll have to dock for repairs."

Dougan grimaced. The crew grumbled, their faces ashen and pale.

Theirs was the most wanted ship in the ocean. Every seafaring nation had designs on her and dreamed of hanging her crew.

The captain looked about in disgust at the fear plastered on the faces of his men.

He paced along the foredeck. They had few options now that the ship was damaged. Where should they go?

There was only one place, one refuge for them now. "We head for the islands, boys! They're our only option and easy pickings to boot."

"We should be heading away from those shores, Captain," yelled old Lob. "Those places be hidin' monsters and strange beasts untold of. There be stories of a monster whale that guards these waters, swallowing ships whole. That very same animal that just rammed us, sir. We should sail away, I say."

The grumbling grew louder.

"Sail west!" a man shouted.

Scrab fired a pistol in the air.

"Enough!" yelled Dougan, slashing his sword in a quick chopping motion to emphasize his authority. The men were afraid; he could feel them yearning for his strength.

Leading a pirate crew was unlike anything else. The men had to be cajoled into every action. Piracy was a kind of grim brotherhood with the captain's iron hand at the helm. "Scrab! How long is the voyage west?"

Scrab looked at Big Billy and shook his head. "We can't stay afloat that long, Captain. We need repairs. Fresh provisions wouldn't hurt neither."

Dougan pursed his lips, tapping the hilt of his sword with long fingers. "We'll squeeze those islands for all they're worth, boys, while our wounded ship is tended to."

Dougan smiled at his crew. "To the islands, the Azores, my boys! Come about!" he yelled. "We'll kill anything that stands in our way and leave their gold-laden churches bare! If that whale dares show again, we blow it out of the seas!"

The men cheered, climbing the riggings and stomping about their tasks on deck.

Scrab shook his head, his eyes foggy.

Dougan raised an eyebrow. "You disapprove?"

"No, hardly." Scrab shrugged.

Talbot walked up behind them, flushed and beaded with nervous sweat.

"Listen," Scrab whispered, placing his ear against the railing "I can still hear it, that creaking sound. It's below us I think."

Dougan felt a vibration, his hand shaking.

"That's no ordinary whale, Captain," said Scrab.

"What is it then?"

"Our ruin," Scrab grumbled under his breath. "We best leave those islands, soon as the ship's put right."

The Dragon scowled, flicking the grime from his boots with a quick motion of his sword. He turned, the men parting way for him, tipping their caps as he made for his quarters. It would be comfortable there, quiet and dark, surrounded by all manner of lovely things: the booty from a hundred ships, long since left to molder, now quiet on the sea bottom.

ANTONIO

He looked out at the water while sharpening his iron harpoon. It was a beautiful thing, the black shaft leading to a broad point that curved up, two jagged edges growing out the side. It was as heavy as it was deadly and it took a strong man to hold and balance the thing on a rocking boat.

Antonio was such a man, large and broad-shouldered. He had been a whaler the whole of his adult life, and not just any whaler. Antonio was a harpooner, the man at the front of the longboat. He was clean-shaven with a square jaw and grim slit for a mouth. A long, white scar ran across his chin, leading up to his cheek. He wore a tight-fitting cap and grey jacket. His clothes were simple and dull; a pair of trousers and a coarse, woolen shirt that had been patched many times over. His dark, reflective eyes peered out from a hard face, and his brown hair curled up from beneath his cap. There was little that was handsome about him, his features strong and leathery. Still, there was kindness in his chiseled face and youthfulness in his playful demeanor.

Antonio was from the Azores, a group of islands in the middle of the Atlantic Ocean. A central spot in the whaling grounds between the old world and the new. Nine emerald jewels set amidst the great blue-grey Atlantic, rising gracefully over its turbulent waves.

He looked aft and saw the distant shape of Pico, one of his nine islands, shimmering ghostly blue in the far off distance. The *Sure Profit,* the ship he served, hunted these waters, always on the lookout for the great whales that migrated around the Azores. Pico's solitary peak—a volcano still known to rumble angrily on occasion—shot up from a halo of clouds. It was an imposing sight, a mountain reaching up from the sea, rising high into an ever-changing sky. He took a deep breath, hoping to catch the scent of the island's rich soil and grapes. The wine grown there was not only enjoyed by the island's peasants, but was also sought after by kings and czars alike. He licked his lips, savoring the memory of its taste.

The *Sure Profit* had been sailing the Azores for a few weeks now, having first docked in Faial for provisions. Faial was home to a great crater with sloping, green hills and high cliffs. From there they had looped around the triangle of islands, filling out their depleted crew with men from the island of São Jorge, a long strip of land with Portuguese settlements clinging to its strangely eroded shoreline. They were tough men, used to isolation and hardship, just like Antonio himself. São Jorge was covered in small huts all along the coast: whale lookouts. When a whale was spotted, the villagers would rush out in their longboats—eager to spear it. This was the lifeblood of the island, their trade and livelihood. Every whaling ship that sailed these parts did the same as Antonio's, scooping up the islanders, cheap and ready for the hunt.

Antonio felt the sharp edge of his harpoon and grunted. This was all he knew. All he would ever know.

"Too long without a whale," said Cabral, the big Cape Verdean. The African was monstrously tall and muscular, with a thick build and black, shining skin.

"Why are you so worried? We've had drier spells before," Antonio mused.

"It's not good to have so little to do," Cabral grumbled.

"What do you mean? There's always something to do onboard this ship."

"I'm here for the whales, Azorean, same as you. I get paid a small share as it is."

"You know, you're always crying about something. Complain, complain, that's all you do." Antonio had a rough voice and a strange, guttural accent. He spoke English well, though the words came out louder and harsher than he intended.

Cabral punched Antonio on the shoulder and gave him a grin. It was a rare sight, as Cabral was surprisingly soft-spoken for his size, and very serious in his manner.

The big African rarely complained, or said much at all. Antonio was the only one he confided in. Cabral had served on many whaling ships, but he never felt at home on the docks of New England or in the company of the English themselves. "You take life too lightly, my friend," Cabral said through a toothy grin.

"Oh, make no mistake, I am worried. If we don't find a big catch soon, Stringer will start to swindle us out of our take. That is a sure thing."

"You should be more careful. You don't want him hearing you speak that way."

"You nag like an old woman. We're harpooners, man! This ship is practically ours," Antonio said, waving his hand in a mockingly royal gesture.

"Murdock's a harpooner, and no one is too fond of him, including the captain. I'd rather not count him as one of us."

Antonio laughed. "True, no one likes that big ape. You know, Jenkins caught him in storage stealing an extra ration."

"What did he do?"

"Jenkins?" said Antonio. "What could he do? The old man has only one hand, poor devil. He spat on the floor and gave the villain one of his angry looks."

"I'd have gutted him," said Cabral, rolling his eyes.

Antonio grimaced. "Don't you talk that way now. You're twice the man he is, no need to prove it."

Cabral shoved Antonio playfully. "Now who's being an old woman?"

Antonio looked down at his harpoons, satisfied. He had about fifty of them to look after. It would often take several to kill a whale, and even if they stuck properly the harpoons could easily peel out of the beast.

"THERE SHE BLOWS! THERE SHE BLOWS!" came the familiar call from the lookout perch.

"Looks like Nesby's spotted one," Antonio said, in surprise.

"A miracle," said Cabral. "I'd be surprised if that boy could find his own backside with both hands."

"Look there! He's right."

Antonio shielded his eyes from the sun and saw a large head in the distance, forming out of the water's surface. The characteristic forward-leaning spout of a sperm whale sprayed out of the creature's blowhole.

"Where away?" came the captain's grumbling voice, as he thumped along the deck in his heavy boots.

"Two miles!" yelled Nesby pointing from his perch. "But, Captain, there's something wrong with it. It's swimming funny."

"Keep your eye on her, boy!"

Captain Stringer rubbed his hands together. He was a short man with a big, white, curling mustache. His eyebrows bowed down over his face, and he had a large, pockmarked nose that glowed red when his temper was up. The men called him "Old Potato" behind his back on account of it. Still, they feared him. Like most sea captains he played the tyrant, and being a whaling captain, he held the ship's promised wealth in the palm of his hand. He took as needed from profits not yet accrued. If a sailor didn't keep good track of what he was owed, he could end up penniless by journey's end.

The *Sure Profit* and its crew of forty had been out of Bedford, New England, for two years now and there were still a hundred barrels to fill. Whales and oil were the only things Stringer cared about, and of course, the coin that came from them.

"It's swimming along the surface in tight circles. Mighty strange," said Antonio, eyebrows raised.

The first mate, Jack Sillings, gripped his arm. He was a gangly, middle-aged fellow with a hooked nose and ginger hair.

"He's a big one, Tony," Jack grinned.

"Maybe it's hurt or protecting a calf?" Antonio guessed.

As the ship sailed towards the whale, the captain cried out, "Stand by and lower away!"

Sperm whales were deep divers; their tails would point straight up before they disappeared into the ocean's depths. This one was hovering just under the surface and hugging the waves.

Five longboats were lowered into the water with their crews, six men each, including one harpooner. The boats were narrow and long, built for speed. With all six men rowing, few things could escape them. Jack was the boatheader at the stern of Antonio's boat. Only mates could handle the steering oar and guide the longboat. It would be Jack's job to guess where the whale would rise again should it dive.

An old New Englander, Jenkins was tireless at the oar, encouraging the other men with his efforts. His mangled left hand still had its thumb and forefinger, just enough to grip an oar.

Three rather soft-spoken sailors were part of the crew: Nesby (barely a man), Ellison (a stout middle-aged fellow with burly arms), and another Azorean named Carlos.

The longboats spread out along the water a quarter mile apart. They would each race towards the whale from a different angle. Cabral raised his oar from another one of the longboats and hooted at Antonio. They would compete for the honor of the first strike.

Murdock was farther away on his longboat, his thick and bristling beard hanging over his chest. He was as tall as Cabral and burly. Antonio thought him the biggest man he had ever seen. Murdock was also crude, with a filthy quality about him. Antonio couldn't help but dislike him from the first.

Where Murdock came from, no one bothered to hazard a guess. It was said he killed a man in Virginia with his bare hands. He wasn't the first criminal to escape on a whaling ship.

It was a rough life, suited for rough men.

The remaining two harpooners, Boots and Zeke, were good men. These two were also from New England, both of them tough, seasoned and good to have at your back in a tight spot. Every one of these whalers had risked their lives time and time again chasing the sea giants. They were all hard and strong men. Antonio had served with many just like them over the years, most long dead.

Antonio grinned as the crews rowed on. It was a grey day, and the winds would help the *Sure Profit* keep pace behind them.

"Keep steady, lads. We'll be on her soon!" shouted Jack as the winds picked up.

As always, old Jenkins began to sing, and the men of the longboats took up the song with him, bellowing as they rowed:

The breeze was fresh; the ship in stays,
Each breaker hush'd, the shore a haze,
When Jack, no more on duty call'd,
His true love's tokens overhaul'd:
The broken gold, the braided hair,
The tender motto, writ so fair,
Upon his 'bacco box he views,
Nancy the poet, love the muse:
"If you loves I as I loves you,
No pair so happy as we two."

This was the moment Antonio loved best. At sea with your mates, rowing strong with a song in your heart. The longboat cut cleanly through the water; waves rolled and splashed over him. The water splattered against his leather coat, and the salty air filled his big lungs as he strained against the oar.

His shoulders adjusted to the rhythm of the pull, and slowly the beast's rippling back came closer into view.

The singing stopped abruptly as they approached the whale. The line of longboats held back collectively. Before them, swimming along the surface with water sputtering out of its blowhole, was a grey and wrinkled monster, a leviathan. Long, white scars covered its body. Dozens of harpoons and spears jutted out of its grey flesh. A horrible white gash ran the length of its blubbery body, peeling and curling outwards. Old, frayed harpoon ropes trailed behind it, like long, parasitic worms. The whale clicked and creaked at the watching whalers, daring them to approach.

"It's him, by God! Old Lazarus!" shouted Jenkins, cackling madly.

"It can't be! He'd be long dead now, an old sea tale," said Jack, raising the steering oar.

"Well, take a good look. What else could that thing be? No ordinary whale, that. They don't call him 'Old Lazarus' for nothing. I told you we would run into him on these waters one day. This beast isn't the only thing guarding these shores. There be monsters here, man, every sailor knows it. Turn around,

Jack. There's no killing this thing," warned Jenkins. "Tell him, Tony! You know this animal. It took your father, man!"

Antonio didn't answer. He was stunned, his heart thundering in his chest. Fear and excitement coursed through him. This whale had haunted his people all his life and haunted his very own nightmares, too. He had been searching for it since first going off to sea. It was thought gone by many, but Antonio's father had spoken often of Old Lazarus, the unkillable beast.

All the old whalers of his village talked of it; a massive bull whale, impossibly big. It had prowled their shores for years, sending scores of ships and men to the bottom of the sea, Antonio's father among them—drowned by the monster when Antonio was still a young boy.

Many sailors had scoffed at the stories. Just the fears of old men, they said.

He was always seeking the whale, hoping to sink a harpoon into the great monster and revenge his old father's death.

"We're whalers, are we not? Think of the oil. The profits. Straight for it then, lads!" Jack shouted.

Antonio was the first to put his oar in the water, praying the beast wouldn't escape him. He looked over at Cabral, and saw the African shaking his head. The men wanted no part of this hunt. This one was too big, too unpredictable and too dangerous.

"Straight for it, lads!" Jack called out again, his voice tense and hoarse.

There was no need to hurry; the whale was still, waiting for them. Only a small portion of its hulking back was still visible on the surface, but this was more than enough to convey its immensity. Its shadow rippled below like some living island as it swam. The whale made a creaking sound, its putrid breath filling the whalers' nostrils.

"Stand up!" Jack shouted from the stern.

It was Antonio's signal. While balancing on the longboat, Antonio reached for his harpoon. The long line fastened to it lay smoothly coiled in a bucket next to his feet. As he stood with his harpoon raised, the whale suddenly lifted its massive tail, spraying the longboats as it spewed from its blowhole. The men braced themselves, fearing the tail would come down on them.

With the waters swirling around it, Lazarus sank and vanished, diving into the deep.

"No!" Antonio yelled.

"Easy, lad. Luck was with us," said Jenkins, wiping the sweat from his brow with his mangled hand.

"What's that out there?" asked Carlos, motioning with a jerk of his head.

Debris floated amidst the swirling waters. In the center of the whirlpool a figure bobbed in the ocean, clinging to something.

"Lazarus must have taken down another ship," Jack gawked.

Antonio lowered his harpoon, and the longboats began rowing towards the body.

"It's a child!" yelled Carlos as they neared it.

It was a boy, in fact, his arms wrapped around a broken door, floating on the waves. A burn or wound of some kind was visible across the left side of his head and shoulder.

The men either crossed themselves or clutched some lucky talisman hidden under their shirts. It was a mighty strange thing seeing a person out here, floating in the middle of nowhere. It could be a sign, an ill omen.

Without thinking, Antonio jumped into the water and swam furiously towards the boy.

"Whoa there, man!" yelled Jack. "That thing is still out there! We need to be ready if it comes back."

Antonio swam alongside the door and hauled the boy off. The longboat caught up and the other whalers swiftly pulled them both aboard.

Antonio was wet and shivering as he was dragged in. Jenkins knelt over the boy, who wasn't responding, and placed his ear to his chest.

"Alive! Wonders, the boy lives," he exclaimed.

Antonio looked down at the boy's naked chest. A gold medallion hung from his neck, the image of a winged angel carved into it. Not a cherub, but an avenging, angry spirit with sword held high. It was the archangel, Saint Michael, namesake of Antonio's home island.

Surely it's a sign, he thought, fumbling with the medallion. Something stirred in Antonio as he looked at the unconscious boy who was pale, helpless and near dead. He traced the raised image on the medallion with his thick fingers. This was providence, a message. Antonio had been taught that God speaks to us in this way, with signs and clues. He felt for this boy, alone with nothing but the image of his patron saint strung around his neck, a victim of the monster whale. Antonio felt sure God put this child in his path. God was speaking to him.

"We have to get him back to the ship. Tom needs a look at him," Antonio urged.

"No. We wait for the whale to rise. We'll need every boat," Jack said.

Antonio grimaced. He had saved Jack more than once out on these seas and the first mate deferred to him in most things, same as most of the crew. The harpooner was a jovial sort, but there was also something solid about him, a sincerity that made the men look to him.

"You would leave him here to die then?" Antonio said, meeting Jack's gaze.

"Alright then," Jack sighed. "We'll take him in. The rest of the longboats will wait here."

Captain Stringer clearly wasn't pleased that a boy was being brought aboard instead of a whale. He stood glaring at Antonio, who carried the limp and unconscious boy in his arms.

"Tom?" Antonio said, staring straight at the captain.

With a nod the captain ordered Antonio below deck, down into the galley to find the strange cook.

The *Sure Profit* had sailed out of New Bedford with a doctor on board, a polite and genial man who constantly took notes and fussed over the men. One year into the voyage he grew melancholy and flung himself off the starboard side. This left Tom, the ship's cook, the crew's only source of medical care.

Tom was remarkably overweight, even for someone who spent his days in the galley. The only hair growing on his head was wisps of blonde curling around his ears. His round face was pimply, and his lazy eye was frozen sideways. Most of his teeth were gone or black, and the hairs on his back sprung out from his collar like golden moss. His white aprons were perpetually filthy, and his belly sagged low over his tight-fitting pants.

"Water is the most important thing," Tom squeaked in his nasal voice.

The cook took a damp cloth and patted the boy's head and cheeks, applying a few drops to his lips.

He was a fair looking boy, with a round face and dimpled chin.

Tom then applied a cloth to the boy's wounds. There was bruising up his shoulder and back. The burn on his forehead glowed red, and raw, dead skin was peeling back along its sides.

"Burns. He was hit by something, I think. Not too deep, though. Should heal well enough," Tom said.

The boy suddenly gasped. He looked up, his expression wide

and fearful.

"No!" he cried.

Antonio reached out, gripping him by the shoulders as he began flinging about.

"Where am I? What is this place?" the boy screamed, looking frantically about the galley.

The room was dark and musky, thick with the scent of overly ripe fruit. Kettles and knives were strewn on the table beside him. The sound of waves lapping against the wooden hull reverberated around them.

"You're on a whaling ship, boy. You're safe," Antonio soothed. "What were you doing out there? We found you alone, floating in the ocean. Did your ship sink? Was it the whale, the monster?"

"I ... I ... don't know," the boy whispered, tears building in his eyes. "I don't ... remember. Where am I?"

Tom tapped his brow as he said to Antonio, "No memory. It might be the injury. A hard blow can do that sometimes."

Antonio peered back at the boy. The child was shaking and looking up at the whaler in confusion. This boy had no past or future, and worse, no understanding of where he was.

"Easy, boy. Easy. Antonio will take care of you," Antonio said.

The boy calmed, his breathing slowing as the panic subsided. Wherever he was, he was safe. The whaler hugged him, holding him tight until he stilled.

"You're safe now, boy," Antonio said. The boy's eyes fluttered, and he fell back into unconsciousness.

Antonio fixed his eyes on the Saint Michael medallion, hanging heavy on the boy's chest. He felt a stirring in his soul. He must protect this boy. God willed it.

THE BARGAIN

The boy woke to a world of darkness and stink with no memory of who he was or where he came from. It was a suffocating blackness, the strange shadows and light of the lamp oil only furthering the boy's confusion and fear.

His head was reeling from the constant sway of the ship, his wounds throbbing with pain. His stomach lurched with each swell of the sea. Sounds of hammering and thudding boots rattled the timbers above and below him, and the ocean's constant crashing filled his ears.

THE WHALEMASTER

Everything seemed held together by ropes and pulleys. It was a crowded world of wood and sail—forlorn and floating, lost on a rolling sea.

Antonio took good care of him, washing his wounds and feeding him bits of salted meat, standard fare aboard ship. Tom fussed over him as well.

The boy spent nearly a week within the blackness of the ship, with no answers for Antonio's many questions.

"No need to worry. Your memory will come back. You had a bump on the head. Your mind is confused. Everything will work out," Antonio soothed.

"What kind of ship is this?" the boy asked.

"This is a whaling ship, my boy, and I am a harpooner. I'll teach you all I know, tell you all my many stories and in return, you'll get better. When your memory comes back we'll find your home. Until then, fear nothing. I'll keep you safe."

Antonio altered some of his own clothing to fit the boy, his big fingers coaxing the needle and thread like an expert seamstress. The hat was oversized, but that suited the boy on cold nights. Antonio, as a harpooner, stayed in steerage and slept in a hard berth along the wall of the ship. A cubbyhole contained all of Antonio's possessions: sewing needle and thread, knife and clothes. Fortunately, there was another berth available for the boy next to him. Antonio had surrendered his pillow and blanket to the boy, sleeping with his jacket wrapped tightly over his big shoulders.

It was hot and stifling within the ship, but Antonio was clearly doing his best to make sure the boy was comfortable. More than once the boy had seen a large black rat crawl past him along the floor. Its movements were slow and ponderous. With no fear of being caught, it strolled royally through the ship's belly.

The other harpooners scared the boy at first. Cabral was grim and silent, always standing beside Antonio with a harpoon at his side. Zeke and Boots would only come down to sleep. When they did appear, they took pleasure in mocking Antonio's fussing.

"A good nurse you would have been, Tony!" they jeered. "Would you tuck me in too?"

The boy grew used to them, all except for the giant, Murdock. The big man would chuckle every time he walked in on the boy. His hairy features and twisted grin made the boy's hair stand on end, not to mention the stench of sweat and rotten fish that always seemed to accompany him.

When Murdock had noticed the medallion hanging around the boy's neck, a strange sneer passed over his grubby face. One night, once the boy had fallen asleep, Murdock's meaty hands reached for the medallion. The boy woke with a start, clutching the saintly image, trying to hold it back against his chest.

"Don't touch." Antonio had appeared noiselessly behind the bully. He gripped Murdock firmly by the wrist.

Murdock pulled his hand away, and stood over Antonio,

glaring down at him in the eerie lamplight. "Touch me again, Islander, and they'll be using you for chum," he growled.

Antonio's face flushed in the darkness and his nostrils flared.

Cabral walked in, glaring menacingly at the hairy giant, his harpoon in hand.

Murdock grinned and strode out, chuckling to himself as he pulled on his greasy beard.

"Keep away from the boy, Murdock!" Antonio yelled after him.

"Stay away from that man," Cabral hissed at the boy. "He is trouble, understand?"

The boy nodded, and Antonio tucked the medallion back into his shirt for the night.

The next day, the boy was finally brought out on deck; the gloomy light stung his tender eyes. Everything seemed grey to him: the ship and its masts, even the sky overhead. The whalers wore grey coats and caps for the most part. The grey ocean seemed alive, foaming and frothing at him. Worst of all was the food, one grey meal following another. Every meal was either salted or dried, accompanied by Tom's "special treat"—a horrible greyish sludge. The boy watched as Antonio did his best to remove the many maggots and bugs that infested it. "Seasoning" was how the crew referred to the pests.

The boy surveyed his surroundings. A brick furnace stood along the ship's deck, two huge cauldrons fixed within it. A container of sorts lay underneath the bricks, to keep the deck from burning when the furnace was lit.

The boy looked up to see six crewmen reefing a sail atop the main mast. Another man stood on a platform looking out to sea, shielding his eyes as he stared out at the horizon. All around the boy were men on their hands and knees scrubbing the deck, as others climbed the rigging. Everyone was quite busy.

An old man stood leaning against the main mast, a large bone of some kind gripped in the remaining thumb and forefinger of his left hand. He was making notches into the creamy white bone with a peculiar-looking tool. He had white hair and thick, woolly sideburns that grew down towards the corners of his mouth. He stared at the boy with pale blue eyes and nodded hello.

"The boy needs a name, Tony," the old man grumbled. "Brings bad luck, not to name something."

The crewmen rolled their eyes, shaking their heads at the old man.

"He has a name, just needs remembering, Jenkins. The poor lad took a blow. Bad luck changing a name too, best wait till it comes back to him."

"A blow! The whale blew him away you mean. 'Twas Lazarus who destroyed the boy's ship and stole his memory," Jenkins said.

The boy looked up at Antonio, confused.

"Enough, old man," Antonio barked.

"Alright, but he'll still need a name if he's to live on this ship. Bad luck otherwise."

"Squid! We should call him Squid," said Cabral.

"Why Squid?" said Boots.

"Squids can kill whales sometimes. Often they strangle the whale and survive being eaten. A fitting name for such a boy." Cabral studied the child for a moment, lifting the boy's face towards him. "They are strange things. I have seen the giant squid, brought up on a net, strangling any in reach of its teeth-filled tentacles. They are thin, transparent creatures, but strong, and difficult to kill. Just like our new friend here. I see it in his eyes, a strong heart, this one."

"I like the name," said Carlos, tossing his long, black locks over his shoulder. The other two oarsmen, Nesby and Ellison, were walking behind Carlos, curious to finally have a close look at the boy.

Carlos walked over and tousled the boy's hair. "You don't look any the worse for wear, do you? It would suit him, this name, I think, no, Tony?"

Antonio laughed and slammed his hand against the boy's back good-naturedly, sending him stumbling forwards a little.

"A good name, a lucky name? Yes, Squid sounds good. What about it?" Antonio said, staring down at the boy for approval.

The boy smiled. If the name made the men happy, who was he to argue?

"What did Jenkins mean, a whale sunk my ship?" he asked,

staring up at Antonio.

Cabral, Jenkins and the other men leaned in, curious to hear Antonio's answer.

"Old Lazarus. A bull sperm whale, a male, you understand? He hunts here, has been a long time, hugging the islands' shores—my islands, the Azores."

Antonio pointed out the island of Flores, a lump in the distance with a rounded, rocky coast. Birds flew overhead, hawks and gulls floating in the sky above the dotted rows of bleached white houses. The faint smell of something sweet seemed to drift in the morning air, and the island shimmered gold-green in the blue horizon. Thousands of flowers, pink and blue hydrangeas, crawled along its many valleys and tall peaks. Corvo, which Antonio said was Flores' sister island, peeked precociously from behind it, a tiny green drop. The little island rose cautiously out of the blue, sheltering behind the larger Flores. Fishing boats bobbed along the Flores coast, colorful little shapes dancing along the water's surface.

"We found you drifting on the water, yes, the last pieces of a broken ship floating everywhere around you. Lazarus was swimming near—that's how we found you. He was eyeing you for a meal no doubt, the devil," Antonio sneered.

He snatched a harpoon from Cabral's hands and held it up.

"The next time we see that monster we'll kill it, empty its guts and avenge your sunken ship! We'll revenge every whaler that's been taken down by that beast. No more will it kill along my homeland's shores."

Cabral rolled his eyes, and Jenkins cackled loudly.

"That's a fool's errand. Won't be an easy kill, that whale. He's as old as the sea and as dangerous, I say," Jenkins croaked.

"It's a whale and we'll kill it, sure as the sun rises. Isn't that right, Cabral?" Antonio grumbled, turning to his friend for reassurance.

"We're whalers. What choice do we have but to go out and lance it? Still, I see little profit in going against that thing. I fear many of us going under in the effort," Cabral said flatly.

"You too?" Antonio said, shaking his head.

"Antonio!" Jack shouted, suddenly, from behind them. "To the captain's quarters with you. And bring the boy."

Jack seemed to avoid Antonio's gaze as he escorted them to the upper deck and the captain's quarters. Antonio knocked on the heavy door and winked at the boy.

"Good luck," Jack whispered, before ushering them forward, the captain staring them up and down as they walked in.

The boy looked around the captain's quarters. They were full of charts and maps. An ugly painting of a woman wearing a blue dress and holding a small dog in her lap hung upon the wall. The woman appeared to be looking down her long nose at him, the ridiculous dog firmly gripped in her strangely long fingers.

The captain was smoking a pipe, the puff rings hovering in the stale air as the pipe bobbed between his teeth. He looked up at them with disdain.

"He can be a ship's monkey, climbing and working the riggings. That's the best I can do for him until we make port on one of the islands, then we can deliver him to the authorities."

"Begging your pardon, sir," said Antonio, clutching at his cap, "but I was hoping the boy could stay with me, in steerage, rather than getting mixed in with the ordinary crewmen. He stands a better chance of finding his place with us there."

"Steerage is for harpooners, Antonio. You get better quarters and a higher share. Isn't that enough? What impertinence, what gall!" the captain growled, tapping his desk with chubby fingers.

Antonio grimaced.

"I can take good care of the boy if he's in steerage," Antonio said, staring at his captain.

"That's not the issue," said Stringer. "This ship is no nursery. He must make himself useful if he wishes to stay."

Antonio placed a hand on the boy's shoulder. "I guarantee he will, Captain."

The boy was making every effort to look strong and capable; he was not confident, however, that he was succeeding.

"I'll train him, sir, if I have to," said Antonio.

Stringer eyed the boy.

"He seems barely out of swaddling clothes to me, and this ship is no place for little children."

Antonio said nothing, placing his big hand on the captain's desk.

Stringer sighed and sank down on his cushioned chair. The captain looked like a man who wasn't used to being argued with, and the boy was surprised he was putting up with Antonio's challenge—Antonio must be of great value to him as a harpooner.

"Very well, he can stay with you in steerage." Captain Stringer sighed. "But there are conditions."

Stringer stared at a metal coin box on his desk. "You'll be paying for his food, clothes and damages incurred by him. Is that clear, Antonio?"

"Done!" Antonio said, grinning. Grabbing the boy quickly by the hand, he began making for the door. The captain called after him.

"Antonio! Think about it, man. Are you sure? Is it worth it? We need a big catch if we're to make up the shortfall. We could be out here another two years yet."

Antonio shrugged. "I saved him, Captain. He's my responsibility. Our fates are tied."

"And what of my lost revenue, Antonio?"

Antonio froze.

"What do you mean, Captain?"

"The whale you gave up for the boy?"

"The men were out there for hours after I came back, Captain. They saw nothing surface."

"No whale can stay under for longer than an hour, Tony," said Stringer, leaning back on his chair. "You know that."

Antonio's jaw clenched and his dark eyes narrowed on the captain's.

"Stay in these waters, Captain. Stay close to my islands. I'll bring you that whale and all the oil your ship can carry. I won't let him get away from me again, my captain, not without lancing him dead. God help me, I swear it."

Stringer nodded. "Very well, Azorean. You've proved your worth thus far."

The boy, who was already being called Squid by most of the crewmen he encountered, woke the next day to Antonio singing a strangely happy and yet mournful Portuguese song. He didn't understand it, but still he was sure the harpooner was belting it out all wrong; it sounded terrible.

"Must we wake every day to your infernal singing, Azorean?" grumbled Murdock.

Antonio sang all the louder, his rich voice reverberating inside the dark ship.

"You must greet the day, boy! There's much to do," Antonio said.

The crew immediately began swabbing the deck upon surfacing. Men with buckets threw cold seawater on the wooden floor, soaking it thoroughly.

Antonio handed Squid a heavy stone and squatted. "Do as I do," he said and began scrubbing hard.

It wasn't long before Squid's back felt as though it would break in two and his arm muscles burned like they were on fire. Antonio smiled when they finished and hauled him up.

Breakfast included a biscuit, along with another of Tom's specialties: pieces of bread boiled with salted meat.

"Tony! There's worms on my biscuit!" Squid exclaimed.

"Glory! Lucky boy! Give it here to your uncle Jenkins," said the old whaler.

"No," said Tony. "Meat's a thing we don't waste on a long voyage. Eat it up."

"I don't think I can," the boy said.

"Fine, try this." Antonio gave Squid his steaming coffee cup. A black sludgy substance curdled on the cup's surface.

Squid tried suppressing the feeling crawling in his stomach and stared at the gazing faces of the crew as they studied him. *Was this some kind of test?*

"Molasses," Antonio chuckled. "It sweetens the drink." The whaler took the biscuit and dunked it in the hot coffee. The worm melted into the black liquid. "Now drink up!"

The boy felt the shriveled worm slide down his throat as he drank the sweet sludge.

"A sailor's delicacy, boy. If we're lucky, one day Boots will catch that rat that's been scurrying about, then we'll have ourselves a fine meal," said Jenkins.

"I draw the line at rats," said Zeke.

"You just haven't tried the right kind of vermin. Curried rat is especially delightful," Boots said, chuckling.

Zeke cupped his hat in his hands and pretended to throw up.

"That's disgusting. Curry is terrible with rat!" said Jenkins.

Cabral was the first to laugh, his head thrown back.

The day was spent hauling in and loosening 'sheets', or sails. The men climbed up ropes to the top of the mast as they swayed and rolled with the ocean. The boy stayed close to Antonio, his stomach lurching with the ship's slightest movements. Fortunately he only vomited twice, bile and biscuit spewing off the side.

"Don't look down, that's the important thing. Just focus on the task at hand and hold tight," Antonio explained.

A rumbling sound was suddenly heard, it seemed to echo from off the sea. Antonio pointed towards a shadow rising from the crimson light breaking along the sea's edge. A whale's square head bobbed out of the water, spewing and sputtering. "A sperm whale! Look how it rises, straight up from the depths. Did you hear its first breath? Nothing like it; you can hear it for miles." Antonio said, patting the boy on the head.

A loud cry went up from the crow's nest. "THERE SHE BLOWS! THERE SHE BLOWS!"

"Come down and see, boy. We'll be going out soon to skewer the beast. Might as well get some practice before we meet Lazarus again." Antonio beamed.

The boy looked out at the creature. *What happened to me out on that sea? Will I ever see my forgotten home?*

He stood transfixed, fascinated. *How could anyone hope to kill such a monster?* he wondered, as fear crawled inside his belly.

SETTING THE CHIMNEY ABLAZE

Squid's gaze followed the longboats, their crewmen rowing hard towards the whale.

The harpooners were all leaning forward on the bows of their boats, anxious to close in on their prey.

Squid noticed a shadow behind him and turned to see Tom, who was looking weary.

"So they've spotted another one, eh? It's been too long since we last brought one in," he grumbled.

"How long will it take them?" Squid asked.

"Could be hours," Tom grunted. "Hopefully that whale

won't dive under as they near him, and hopefully the harpoons land well into him, deep and hard. Sharp as the harpoons are, often they fall away as the whale swims or jumps up in anger."

Squid heard the whalers' song, bellowing from the longboats as they skimmed through the waves.

"Why do they sing like that? What's the point?" asked Squid.

Tom shrugged. "I have no idea. Tony says it's to drive out the fear."

"Fear of the whale?" Squid asked.

"Yes, and more besides. Oftentimes the boat gets overturned, and the men aboard have to wait for ship and rescue. Many have drowned that way, and if we happen upon an especially feisty whale, heaven help the men aboard a longboat."

"But Tony isn't really afraid, is he?"

"No, and if he is he don't show it," said Tom. "He's been killing whales a long time, that islander. No one is better at it."

There was enough wind for the ship to keep up; they were not too far behind the longboats. The whale swam and dove in a kind of heavy rhythm in front of them, snorting from its blowhole, oblivious to the menace rowing fast towards it. It jumped out of the water at first sight of the whalers, crashing against the waves playfully.

Antonio's longboat kept pace with it, the crew rowing behind the whale. Bringing up his knees, he leaned forward. Soon the animal would be within striking distance. The men grew silent as they pulled on the oars.

Antonio sprang up with his big harpoon. The iron shaft protruded from a wooden pole in Antonio's hands, the point hanging menacingly off of the bow. The harpooner stood tall and still like a statue, the boat cutting through the water.

Antonio heaved with his big arm and the harpoon sailed out of his hands, embedding itself firmly within the beast's flesh. The iron shaft sunk into the white blubber, blood spewing in inky globs from the whale's rippling hump and into the churning water.

"STERN ALL!" yelled Jack from starboard.

Antonio sent another harpoon into the whale as the rowers frantically backed the boat away from the massive tail, which was now rising angrily above them. A rope unraveled from the longboat, spinning from the bobbing harpoons.

Murdock's longboat came alongside Antonio's. The big man rose up and threw his own harpoon at the whale. The beast flailed as more of its blood tinted the red waters.

"Something is wrong," said Squid instinctively, watching the anxious expressions of the whalers.

The two boats were being dragged, jerking from side to side as men fell sprawling. Screams were coming from Antonio's longboat. Squid could just make out the figure of someone kicking, the cries of pain carrying over the water. Jenkins was fumbling nervously over a struggling figure.

"Damn!" Tom cursed. "Someone's come too close to the unraveling rope. The strength of the whale's pull causes great friction. Whalers can lose an arm or leg to that rope. You've seen Jenkin's poor hand? He's felt the rope's sting."

"Who's hurt?"

"One of the young ones, I think, one of the New Englanders."

The screams became sharper and shrill as the ship neared the struggling longboats.

"I need to go," said Tom, looking ashen and grey. "Oh, to be just a plain cook again." Tom patted the boy on the shoulder and shuffled away.

It was a large sperm whale, a red mist trailing after as it dove into the ocean. The ensnared longboats continued to get pulled forward and the ropes spun out in a hiss. The crews of the other three longboats rowed calmly alongside the ship, and the little fleet waited for the whale to resurface.

After a moment, the sperm whale erupted out of the water, the harpoons still spiked into its wrinkled body. It made an agonized creaking sound as it slapped the water with its tail.

Oarsmen on both the fastened longboats poured water on the whizzing ropes. The heat was causing them to smoke as they spilled out from their spools.

The longboats were keeping their distance from the tortured animal. In the water around the whale floated crimson gore.

Squid could see the men with more detail now. They looked on impassively at the dying animal. This was their trade, nothing more. They had no pity for the noble beast dying before them.

Squid recognized the moans coming from Antonio's longboat. It was indeed Nesby, clutching at his arm. The whalers grimaced, shaking their heads as if it was no surprise to them. They had seen this before. It looked as though Nesby was lucky he hadn't been killed right off by the rope.

Antonio stared at the rope as it rolled out, the spool growing smaller and smaller, his axe raised as if ready to cut the rope if need be.

The whale stopped its thrashing abruptly and gave out an exhausted groan. Its body heaved as it bled and breathed a last, agonized breath. It was in its final death throes. The rope held as the longboats closed in for the kill.

The whale rolled sideways, its jaw flapping loose, its bulging eye staring out at the ship. Squid thought it was staring right at him, pleading with him in some way.

To Squid's surprise, it wasn't Antonio who finished off the poor animal. It was Jack, the first mate. With a long spear he jabbed at the whale. First once, and then several times. Squid guessed he was looking for an essential organ. All of a sudden, a wide spray of blood gushed into the air, like a fountain, from the whale's pulsing blowhole.

Squid had heard the whalers speak of this. They called it "setting the whale's chimney ablaze" or "raising the red flag." The blood came out thick and strong at first, spilling over the creature's head. The air filled with the smell of iron and blood. With a final shudder the great whale died, floating limp and motionless.

What a horrible way to die, thought Squid.

Antonio and Cabral hopped on another longboat and carried Nesby back to the ship as soon as the whale stilled. The other men moved in with ropes and hooks. Murdock gave the whale's hide a celebratory kick as if making sure the thing was really dead.

Nesby was pale and moaning. What was left of his bloody arm was pressed tight against his red-stained shirt. The rope had tangled around his arm and severed it clean above the elbow. He gave Squid a sad smile, and then collapsed on deck in front of him, blood traveling and pooling around Squid's feet.

"Pick him up!" yelled Antonio. "Hurry. He's losing too much blood!"

A rag had been tied above the wound and Antonio struggled to tighten it.

"Get him down to Tom before it's too late!" he shouted.

Squid ran up and helped pick Nesby up. The young man's eyes were rolling into the back of his head and his skin was turning blue before Squid's eyes.

Nesby's hat fell off his head, and he looked much younger than Squid had first thought. He had a thin, boyish face with an upturned nose and dimpled chin. He must have been only a few years older than Squid himself, sixteen or seventeen at the oldest.

They ran down the steps towards the galley, Squid holding up Nesby's quivering legs.

"Keep him up off the ground! Keep him up and tilted," Cabral shouted. The Cape Verdean's eyes glowed white in the darkness and his black face streamed with shining sweat as he called out Nesby's name.

"Stay with me, Nesby!" Antonio screamed.

Tom was pouring sand on the floor to keep from slipping on the blood. There was a cleaver, saw and pot of boiling water beside him.

"Place him on the table," Tom huffed.

"Don't take my arm. Please don't take it," Nesby pleaded.

"Your arm's already gone, boy," Antonio frowned, gripping Nesby by the shoulder.

"Hold his feet down," Tom instructed.

Cabral grabbed Nesby's feet, tight under his strong arm.

"Squid, hold Nesby's other arm. Keep it pinned, understand me?" Tom said.

Squid went pale, but nodded.

"Here, drink this, boy," said Tom producing a bottle of rum from his pocket. He placed it against Nesby's lips and forced it down his throat, causing the young man to choke and heave. "That's it, all the way down."

Nesby turned and faced Squid, a desperate expression on his blue-grey face.

"Don't let them take it," he pleaded.

Squid gripped Nesby's hand. "Don't worry. Everything will be alright now. We'll fix you."

Squid looked over at Antonio for reassurance, the harpooner turning from his gaze.

"He's lost a lot of blood already," Tom croaked.

The galley filled with Nesby's screams as pitch and flame were forced into his oozing wound. Tom had no knowledge of arteries or surgery. Fire was the only way he knew of to stop the wound from bleeding.

Squid shut his eyes tight and put his full weight against Nesby's struggling arm. Tom backed away and took a swig from the rum bottle, wiping the trails of sweat off his protruding brow.

"Done," gasped the fat cook.

Antonio and Cabral relaxed, and Squid opened his eyes to see Nesby looking back at him.

"I should have never come on this ship," he whispered. "I only wanted to see the world."

Suddenly Nesby's body began convulsing and pinkish foam bubbled out of his mouth.

"No! No!" Antonio yelled, flinging himself over Nesby's body, trying to still him. "Stay with me, boy!"

Nesby let out a hiss and his body went loose.

Antonio grabbed the hat from off his head, eyes moistening in the oily lamplight.

Squid gawked at Antonio. He hadn't imagined the strong

harpooner was capable of tears. Antonio's shoulders were trembling, his sorrow uncontainable.

Cabral walked over, embracing his friend. "He was a brave boy," he muttered sadly.

"I should have cut the rope," Antonio hissed. "I should have let the whale go!"

"Would have made little difference," Tom said. "He didn't bleed out. It was the shock and strain of his wound."

Tom took another swig from his bottle and covered Nesby's face with a rag.

Antonio wiped his eyes and walked out, Cabral motioning for Squid to follow.

The boy felt numb, sickened by what he had just seen and more than a little afraid.

They climbed up the narrow stairs, Squid shadowing Antonio's heavy slow steps. "Why do you hunt the whales, Tony?" he asked hesitantly. "Why do it if you could die?"

Antonio shrugged before lifting the hatch and entering the light. He stood and stared off in the direction of his islands, his eyes red and teary. "It's what we do. What other life is there for a poor islander?"

Antonio placed his arm around Squid's shoulders, looking down at the dead whale and surrounding longboats, all bobbing in the reddening water.

The whalers were preparing the beast's body for lashing up along the side of the ship, making a hole near its eye for a good spot to hook it.

With a sinking feeling Squid realized the creature's dead gaze reminded him of poor Nesby. *What am I doing here?*

TRYING-OUT

I said, I will take heed to my ways: that
I offend not in my tongue.

I will keep my mouth as it were with
a bridle: while the ungodly is in my sight.

I held my tongue, and spoke nothing:
I kept silence, yea, even from good words;
but it was pain and grief to me.

My heart was hot within me, and while
I was thus musing the fire kindled: and at
the last I spoke with my tongue;

Lord, let me know mine end, and the
number of my days: that I may be certified
how long I have to live.

— **PSALM 39**

The whalers stood swaying with the rocky deck, caps off as Stringer mumbled his prayer. He read the words from his black bible, coolly flipping its delicate pages with his swollen fingers.

Antonio and Squid had prepared Nesby's body, sewing him inside a grey canvas shroud. A heavy iron pot was placed at his feet and sewn in with him to help the body sink. At Jenkin's insistence the last stitch went through the corpse's nose, as was custom.

"Best make sure he's dead. Every sailor deserves that final courtesy," the old whaler croaked.

Antonio stood with his eyes shut, muttering prayers and spinning the beads of his rosary along thick fingers. With a final "amen," Antonio and Cabral stepped forward, hoisting the body over the railing and dropping it into the sea.

Nesby bobbed on the surface for a moment, the waters still bloody from the whale's carcass. Then he sank with a gurgle and was gone.

Jack blew a whistle and the men returned to their gruesome work. Cabral clapped Antonio on the back. Antonio put away his rosary, folding it into his pocket.

Antonio placed his cap back on his head and rested a hand on Squid's shoulder, then joined the others, somberly moving towards the whale.

The body of the whale was hoisted by the head and fastened to the side of the ship. Gulls flew overhead, squawking and pecking at the dead beast's wrinkled skin. Then the whalers began cutting into the whale's flesh with their tools; the flensing had begun.

Flensing involved removing large chunks of the whale's skin or blubber with sharp spades. The long strips of oily blubber were lifted by rope and lowered into a hatch that led to the blubber room below deck.

This was the workroom of the ship, where large blanket pieces of blubber were cut into smaller pieces and sent back up to the trywork furnace.

Squid watched as the heavy strips were removed from the whale, a long stream of gore spewing into the ocean, as sharks calmly circled the ship.

Antonio seemed especially adept at using the sharp spades that cut up the whale, his arms rippling as he swung. The work was slow but steady, the whalers singing with each chopping motion. Eventually there was nothing left of the whale but some meat, bones and a gargantuan, square head. Antonio and the whalers climbed on what was left of the whale and hacked at the remaining neck. When finally removed, the head was placed on deck with its long jaw hanging limp.

The teeth were carefully removed and piled neatly to one side. A hole was cut into the head so its highly prized substance, spermaceti, could be removed with a bucket. It was white and waxy, and used for making candles and fancy cosmetics.

"The candles never drip and burn a brilliant light. They cost more than any whaler here could afford, except our dear captain. If we're lucky we'll find ambergris, and the captain will dance a happy jig," Jenkins laughed.

Antonio had told Squid that ambergris was sometimes found in the lower intestine of the beast, and was used was for perfume and even believed to have healing properties. However, as much as Antonio searched and carved into the carcass, there was none to be found.

"Shame, the captain's mood will darken and we will all be the poorer," old Jenkins grumbled.

"Isn't all this blubber and oil enough?" Squid asked.

"Huh!" exclaimed Jenkins. "All the whales in the seven oceans wouldn't be enough, boy. Oil means light and fancy goods for the rich and dainty. The world hungers for it, lad. If not us, then someone else would be here, probing and peeling this poor creature for its treasure."

"Why do you do it, Jenkins?" Squid said. "Why are you here?"

"Why? I was born for this life at sea! Served under every kind of tyrant captain, I have, manning the sails and scrubbing their bloody decks. Better to be a harpooner, standing tall on the longboat, I say."

"Were you a harpooner, Jenkins?" Squid gasped.

"I was indeed. Until my accident," said Jenkins holding up his mangled hand. "'Twas a big one too. A right whale, covered in barnacles and tiny sea creatures, she was. The boat cracked in half and the rope swung free, taking most of my hand. I felt no pain. A clean cut, it was."

Jenkins sighed. "That's the life, boy. Hard and free, no better life for a man."

Squid shook his head. "There're many ways to live your life, I'm sure, and be happier than this?"

"Happy!" Jenkins hooted. "Is that life's purpose, boy? You've been spending too much time with that clowning Portuguese islander."

Jenkins turned and looked at Antonio, still cutting into the whale's head with his spade.

"For all his fooling, he's the best, I think. No one better in a pinch. I've never seen the iron wielded so well. Damn Azoreans seem born for it!" Jenkins slapped his knee and chuckled. "He has the devil's instinct for where the whale will surface, and his harpoons sink well into the whale's hide, hard and true."

"You like him because he's a good harpooner?"

"No, boy, you miss the point." Jenkins eyes narrowed on Squid, his bushy sideburns blowing white against his wrinkled old face. "It's a test, you see. There's no middle ground here, no room for slow thinking. The sea is always daring, calling out to a man, taunting. Most men spend their lives trying to find themselves. Am I a coward, a good man or a bloody villain? The sea will tell you, boy. Give your life to her and she'll tell you, true. And if you miss a step she'll send you down below." Jenkins smiled. "God lives out here, judging and testing us all. He takes what he wishes, even good young men like our dear Nesby, and in the end all he offers is truth. The real answers, boy. The things that make a man whole."

Jenkins pointed to Antonio. "Tony knows that. He takes life as it comes and carries more than his own load on his back. He's got sea water running right through those veins. Stay close to him and you'll learn what kind of man you are, or should be, that is. Not to say he isn't without strangeness. All them Azoreans be a little touched, to my mind. Melancholic they are, singing and laughing one minute, and then closed off and silent like the next. Sentimental, a little foolhardy, stubborn and tough as old shoe leather, that's how I'd describe those islanders. Broke the mold when they made that one, though, big brute."

"Do you think he'll kill Lazarus, the monster?" Squid asked, suddenly feeling flushed, imagining the great whale's head propped up against the ship.

Jenkins simply frowned and stared to starboard at a misty, volcanic island he told Squid was called Graciosa, the enchanted isle and northern rock of the Azores. Its green hills sloped gently into the sea, stone hamlets spreading across its hillsides in neat little patterns, crawling up its many ridges and emerald veins. The outlines of a volcano, a great crater, yawned from the southwest of the pretty island. A church bell rang out in the distance, echoing from sandy, white shores.

The ship had seemed to hug the archipelago for weeks, daring the great whale to come out and meet it. "Best be getting back to work, boy," Jenkins said, and turned to join Antonio, who was still cutting at the whale.

By nightfall the furnace was lit and the two massive try-pots set boiling. Thin, rectangular pieces of blubber that the whalers called bible leaves were fed into these pots until all the oil was leeched out of them. The fires and smoke blazed through the night, illuminating the faces of the bloodstained whalers. They called boiling out the oil from the blubber "trying-out."

The oil was stored in barrels. Having been heated to high temperatures, it would never spoil.

"Not good enough," Squid heard Captain Stringer exclaim, as he fed the fiery cauldrons. "We could be out here for years yet before filling the rest of our quota!"

"The men are nervous, sir. They say we should try our luck elsewhere," Jack hissed. "Old Lazarus spooked them—you know the stories. We sail too close to these shores. The men want no part of this, Captain."

"Bah! Not Antonio. He's willing to take the beast on. That whale was the largest we've seen yet. I must have him, Mr.

Sillings. Our backers would demand no less of us."

Jack nodded curtly and the captain strode away, muttering angrily to himself.

The thick, black smoke of the tryworks obscured the riggings and trailed past the ship, swirling in the grey sky overhead. The whalers were covered in blood and grease, giving them a grisly appearance. What remained of the whale carcass was cut loose, and the circling sharks and gulls feasted all the more.

Antonio had grown quiet after Nesby's death and kept Squid close. The two hovered near the ship's bubbling, black cauldrons.

"I don't think it was your fault, Antonio," said Squid tentatively.

"Whose was it, then? He was on my boat. I should have been more careful. Damn the coin, I should have cut the whale loose," Antonio huffed.

The heat from the cauldron made Squid wince. Sweat poured down his brow. He looked up at Antonio's sad features. The heat didn't seem to bother the big whaler much at all.

"Jack wouldn't have let you."

Antonio sighed. "No, I suppose you're right. The boy knew the dangers when he signed aboard. I won't let it happen again, though. Coin and captain be damned."

"And Lazarus?" Squid whispered.

Antonio stared at him, eyeing the scar on Squid's forehead. The gash that had run from his hairline down towards his eye had healed well.

"I've heard tell of Lazarus since I was a child. The villagers fear him, and pray for the whalers whenever they go out to sea. They prayed for my father too, for all the good it did him. That beast didn't even leave a body for me to mourn, took the old man down below with him." Antonio placed his hand on the boy's head, ruffling his cap. "It took your ship, Squid. You're all that's left of it. I fear your parents are gone, it hurts to say, but I think so. I think Lazarus is evil, Squid. I have to kill him, before he kills again. That's why I'm here, why you were sent to me."

Antonio gulped. "That amulet around your neck—you know whose image is on it, don't you?"

"Saint Michael, who drove the devil, the dragon, out of paradise," Squid answered, wondering where the story's memory had come from.

"On my island there is a large statue of that very same angel. He's our saint; the island is named after him, São Miguel. It's a sign, you see. We're tied together, like the angel and the dragon. I have to kill the devil whale now or more ships will go down."

Antonio shrugged. "What were you doing on that ship anyway? Do you remember anything of your parents yet?"

Squid had the faintest image of a woman in white, walking on a slippery deck in her bare feet.

He looked up at the whaler and shook his head. "No, but I know I'm alone. I feel it. There's no one waiting out there for me," he said.

Antonio pulled the boy close. "You're not alone. Antonio's here." The harpooner's lips curled into a broad, crooked smile.

"Are you alone, too, Tony? Do you have any family left?"

"My mother died when I was young. My only memory is of a sick woman, coughing out her life in a little stone hut. Other women came, dressed in black as they always do when someone dies. They pray forever on my island, it seems. It's a constant thing, like the tide." Antonio frowned, and continued, "My father was a good man, a good whaler. He taught me what it means to be a real man." Antonio waved his hand in a grand gesture over the distant island of Graciosa.

"My village is not far from here, Squid. I sailed these waters as a boy, fishing and playing in the sea." Antonio chuckled. "These islands hold many memories for me; I know them like the back of my hand, and still they surprise. Each one unique, beautiful and cruel in its own way." Antonio shook his head. "To be Azorean is to be torn in two, your soul caught between these strange little lands and the fickle sea."

Antonio scowled. "What kind of life is that anyway; to scrub at the earth for morsels, living in poverty? Better to take a chance at sea, live as a free man. This was what I thought then."

Squid looked up at Antonio and felt a stab of pity for the big man, recognizing the harpooner's loneliness.

Antonio shook his head slowly, regretfully. "Perhaps when we land for provisions we can visit my village, and plan a better life for us both. But not before I fulfill my promise and kill that devil whale. I'll do what my father couldn't, and drive that thing back to hell. My aim is true; he won't escape me again."

That night, in the darkness of his cubbyhole, Squid heard the sound of distant thunder. It boomed somewhere far off, mingling with the sounds of the rolling waves.

The woman came to him in his dreams, her long, white dress and black hair floating in the water as she reached out to him. She was pale and beautiful, her slender form twisting underwater as she swam to him. She called his name, but he could not hear it. A loud creaking sound rippled all around him. From below an enormous, swollen eye came up, peering at him. And then he woke to the sound of heavy footsteps thumping on the timbers above.

The harpooners leapt out off their cubbyholes and ran above deck, towards the commotion.

Antonio grabbed a harpoon and hauled the boy out of bed.

"Come on," said Antonio, blinking the sleep out of his eyes.

The crew and captain were all huddled at the starboard side of the deck, staring off at an approaching ship.

It was a two-masted vessel with square riggings. A white flag flew over her, red at her topmast, which was a signal of distress.

"Antonio!" Jack shouted. "We've been signaling at her with no answer. I'll need someone to go aboard with me when we come alongside."

"Aye, I'm your man," Antonio said. "I'll take Cabral and Ellison."

"I want to come too," Squid mumbled.

"No, boy. You stay here with Jenkins."

Squid turned, finding old Jenkins smiling at him with yellow, stained teeth, waving his two fingers.

The approaching ship looked empty with no motion or sound coming from within her. She didn't seem anchored, just drifting hapless.

Squid caught a shape draped over the ship's railing and a long red smear flowing from it. "Antonio, look there! I see something," he said.

A body hung limply off the ship's port side, blood staining the ship's hull in ribbons.

"Dear God," Cabral said, crossing himself.

The captain nodded towards Jack, and the wayward ship was grappled and brought alongside. Cabral and Antonio were the first to jump over. Jack held a pistol; Squid could see it shaking in the first mate's hand.

Squid couldn't see over the ship's deck; he could only make out the tops of the whalers' heads as they moved about.

"God in heaven! What on earth happened here?" he heard Jack shout.

Something was stretched across the ship's wheel. Squid climbed the riggings for a better view and saw a headless body tied across it, its arms spread out and dangling.

The bodies of the crew were butchered, piled together in a mass along the bow of the ship.

"Bodies everywhere, Captain!" Jack shouted, looking ashen and pale. "They're all dead! Every last one of them."

"Whoever did this tied the captain to the wheel, headless. It's a ghastly sight, sir," Antonio barked.

Stringer's mustache quivered as he rubbed his damp forehead. "Check below for survivors and hurry off that ship. I want away from the thing!" he shouted.

"What do you make of this, Captain?" Jack turned towards the whaling ship and held up a flag for the captain to see.

Squid froze as Jack held up the bloody flag. He had seen its image somewhere before, a black dragon in a field of red. His head began to ache.

The memory of another ship entered his mind, a sinking ship with masts aflame. Through the black smoke the same red flag burned through his thoughts, the black emblem snarling.

A sickly sweet smell filled his nostrils; he wasn't sure if it was from the *Sure Profit* or the dead-filled ship they were tethered to.

"It's the Dragon!" said Jenkins below him. "He's returned to these waters."

Squid stared at the old man. "Who's the Dragon?"

"He's exactly what we don't need, boy. Another monster."

SCRIMSHAW

I t was a strange life inside the belly of the whaling ship. The forecastle was dark and cramped. The heat was stifling. The rank smell of sweat hung heavy in the stale air. Trunks and baggage lay everywhere on the greasy floor. Pipe smoke drifted above the cackling mad crew. The atmosphere was suffocating, and the small entrance hatch above was the only source of daylight and fresh air. Squid hung below it in effort not to get sick.

Filthy pots and pans hung in tight corners. A chicken strode along the filthy, black floor, clucking and scratching.

Antonio had decided to take Squid to join the men for the evening. A generous cup of rum swirled in Antonio's big hand.

It had been a bloody day. The corpse-filled ship had shaken the whaling crew, casting a grim silence over all of them during the long day. So, they did the only thing they could with the night: they sang, drank and danced on their bone-weary legs.

"I miss Nesby!" said a staggering Zeke, his red cap tilted precariously on his head.

"Aye! The boy could jig and hop with the best of them. Funny monkey, he was," said Jenkins.

"Play something happy, Ellison! A foot stomper!" yelled Boots.

Ellison gave a wide grin. He took up a fiddle and the whalers' faces glowed. Crewmen jumped out of their cubbyholes and Squid's feet tapped to the sounds of the pipe and fiddle, almost without his notice.

"Why is everyone so happy? I don't see any reason for it, especially after today," Squid said, squinting and wheezing from the smoke.

"Why not? What else is there to be?" Antonio said, gulping down his burning cup of rum.

Two men began fighting under the stairs. Boots walked up, throwing them off each other. Everyone roared with laughter at the pair's drunken and bloody faces.

"Where's Cabral?" Squid asked.

"He's a grump! Sulking somewhere beside his harpoon, most

likely." Antonio chuckled.

Men took each other arm in arm and spun about, hooting and stomping heavily on the floor.

Antonio slapped his knee in time to the music, all the while toasting the fiddler and chugging his rum. After a time Antonio's face slackened, red and drooping with the drink. His eyelids hung heavy and his movements turned slow and ponderous. His strength seemed sapped, and a pathetic quality hung over his big, slumping frame. He smiled crookedly up at Squid, who couldn't help but feel a little sad, disappointed even, in his protector.

A man slipped, and the room erupted in jeering calls. The faces of the whalers took on an eerie glow in the candlelight.

Antonio's head bobbed crookedly with the music. Squid shook his head and climbed up towards the open deck.

He looked up at the stars blanketing the night sky, a moonless night with the cosmos shining down at him.

"A grand night, boy," said Jenkins, climbing up behind him. "The Whalemaster has had a few too many, I think."

"He's upset, but he won't say it," muttered Squid.

"Aye! Who wouldn't be?" groaned Jenkins.

The whalers were belting out a thunderous tune below, their stomping rattling the timbers that held the deck together. Squid could hear Antonio's voice carrying over the others, torturously out of key.

While up the shrouds the sailor goes,
Or ventures on the yard,
The landsman, who no better knows,
Believes his lot is hard;
But Jack with smiles each danger meets,
Casts anchor, heaves the log,
Trims all the sails, belays his sheets,
And drinks his can of grog.

"Ha! A great harpooner he may be, but a right awful singer. Never could handle his liquor neither," said Jenkins, laughing.

Squid, in no mood for fun, ignored him. The try-pots were still blazing, the orange fire playing off Cabral's dark face. He stood there watching the fires, lost in thought.

"Best to leave him, lad," Jenkins whispered. "That big African is not up for socializing just now. He's been in a dark mood since boarding that ship."

"I can understand that. Those poor people were slaughtered. The singing and dancing makes no sense to me."

"A whaler must numb himself to slaughter. It's our trade in a way."

"Not regular people though. No one could get used to a sight like that."

"No, not regular people, whoever they are." Jenkins shrugged. "I dare say the crew's more rattled than they let on. It's the way of men sometimes. To bury themselves in drink and song, warding off the gloom and fear that clamps down in their insides."

"You said it was a monster that killed those men. A dragon?"

"Oh yes, the most fearsome of them: a man, flesh and bone. Lord William Dougan, the bastard. Scourge of the Atlantic and pirate captain of the *Red Gull*. A golden-haired and ruthless dandy he is, with two hundred cutthroats at his command. Lord William Dougan is tall and regal like a right proper noble with cool manners and fancy dress. Cuts a fine figure in a blood-red uniform. His eyes shine blue like the raging sea and smiles, he does, a handsome smirk. He laughs, you see, quite happily, as he guts you."

"So, he is evil? Like the whale? Have you seen him yourself?"

"Seen him? Up close? Heavens, boy, I'd be dead if I had. Evil, you say? Yes, he trades in death and gold," Jenkins grumbled. "He's dashing, yes, but pitiless cruel. A right proper 'gentlemen' he is too, well trained in the sword. Like all those rich English bullies, feeding off us poor, honest folk. Made him famous it has, though, one end of the world to the other."

"But you said he was a bastard. How can he be a lord?"

"He isn't, really. It's a joke, you see. His father was a wealthy, important man, but Dougan was never really wanted. Unloved, he was. So, deprived of fortune, he took to a life at sea, taking his past wrongs out on the world."

"That's sad."

"Sad? Everyone has a sad story, boy. Look at my hand," said

Jenkins, holding up his fingers. "Everyone has scars of some kind, even you. Some too deep to see."

Jenkins shook his old head. "Besides, he's not the only one on that ship to worry about. There's Scrab."

"Scrab? What kind of name is that?"

"One for a devil. Probably hatched straight out of hell, he was. No blacker figure has ever sailed these seas. No one knows who Scrab is or where he came from. Some say he served the cursed royal navy, and like many, deserted for the freer life of piracy. Others say he was a prisoner. Locked away in some dark tower, he escaped before his deserved hanging. Clad head to toe in black he is. With a face as old and wrinkled as a sperm whale's hump, and uglier to boot. A Spaniard captain took his leg just as Scrab was about to take his ship. Scrab had that captain skinned, they say, his screams reaching as far as the Bahamas."

Squid's head hurt, and he braced himself against the ship's railing.

"Are you alright, boy? You've been as pouty and strange as Cabral lately."

"Maybe it's those bad stories you keep telling, old fool!" Cabral cursed loudly, still facing the fire.

"I don't tell bad stories. I tell great ones, with only a slight embellishment here and there," Jenkins blustered.

Cabral groaned and picked up his harpoon to leave.

"Don't pay him no mind, boy. Dull-witted he is," Jenkins

whispered.

"Call me that again and you'll be the one who's skinned, old man!" Cabral yelled from the darkness.

"Huh? Good hearing though. Damn Cape Verdeans, great whalers in general, but a might touchy."

"You think they'll be able to hear your screams from Cuba?" Cabral barked.

"Not Cuba you heathen brute, the Bahamas!" Jenkins yelled back.

Cabral grunted and stomped down below deck, the trap-door slamming behind him. Jenkins stuck his tongue out after him and Squid smiled despite himself.

"I've been watching you, lad. You're a good boy. A natural. The captain's no fan though," Jenkins warned.

"I don't mind. I think he's a little afraid of Antonio."

"A little, yes. The fool's worried about the profits, always the profits. No Antonio, no whale. He's the best harpooner we've got and the most experienced. We all owe money to that bloated-sack-of-wine captain. I'll be lucky to get a shilling when this is all over. We have to buy everything in advance. Every cloth and stitch, sometimes even the food we need from our hard earned provisions."

Squid looked up at the stars again. He rubbed the scar on his forehead, the wound aching in the cold.

"Ah, the stars, they sparkle, they do, take on a life of their own by these Azores. And why shouldn't they? We're in the middle of nowhere, ain't we, my boy? Between worlds it seems. Come with me. I have something for you," Jenkins said, suddenly grabbing the boy by the arm.

Squid followed towards the bow of the boat. Amidst the barrels lay a tarp, heaped along the timbers. Jenkins removed it and gestured with pride at a pile of bones and enormous teeth.

"Scrimshaw," Jenkins exclaimed. "It's new! An islander taught me. It's a real art, boy! Carving into the whalebones, make an image of any kind, I can."

Jenkins handed Squid a large tooth with a ship carved into it. The waves were carved in ripples and swirls looping around the image of the tilting vessel, the lines quite subtle in places. The notches had a surprising depth and realism. The carvings imparted to the hard tooth a delicate and beautiful transparency.

Squid stared down at the motley collection of whalebones. Carved ships, figures and sea creatures danced in the furnace light.

"They're wonderful!" Squid gasped. "How do you do it, with your hand and all, I mean?"

"Ain't nothing, boy. I grip the bone with my bad hand, and carve using the good. With this tool here." Jenkins produced a small iron shank with a whalebone handle, every bit as full of intricate designs and patterns as the pieces it carved.

"Here," Jenkins said, grabbing a tooth and placing it in the boy's small hand.

It was half the size of his palm and yellowed, a brown stain blemishing the one side. Squid turned it over and saw an image of a whale carved into it.

Its jaw was open and men swam around it, floundering in the water. Amidst the patterns and carved waves a ship lay broken and sinking. A longboat floated before the whale; a man stood with a harpoon raised at its bow. A long gash was cut into the whale's side.

"It's Lazarus, isn't it?" the boy gasped, staring at it with awe.

"Yes. Hold on to it, boy."

"Why did you carve it?"

"I don't know. When I finished I thought of you, though. I think you're meant to have it."

"Do you think he took my family? My ship?"

"Probably, but something tells me there might be more to it. Sometimes these sea creatures and people become tied together somehow. I knew a whaler who was saved by a whale once. Near drowning, he was, and a whale carried him up close to shore, safe and sound. He met the whale again, years later, only at the end of his harpoon. He never sailed again after that, fearing the deed had tainted his mortal soul. Swore fate would drown him the next time he set foot on a longboat, just like old Jacinto, Tony's dear dad."

"You knew him?"

"Sure I did. Sailed with the sea dog more than once. Much like his son, with Cabral's dark humor. Most ships sailing these waters make a stop by these islands, shore up their crews with the Azoreans. Tony's well sought after. Real prince he is amongst our rough sort."

Squid gripped the tooth and felt the carved impression.

"Thank you, Jenkins. I'll take good care of it," he gulped.

"Take care of yourself, boy. Even with Antonio looking out for you, the sea is a fickle, old thing. I hope that tooth offers some luck. Maybe we'll sail by these islands easy and never see that cursed whale again."

Squid gave Jenkins a strange look, the image of the woman flashed in his waking mind. The whale's long creaking echoed in his thoughts.

"Maybe," the boy said, shuddering at the black night sea, at the stars reflecting in the murky depths.

WOLVES OF THE SEA

The food had improved slightly. Squid savored the meat. Tom, who favored the boy, had prepared this morsel special, just for him. The portly galley cook had some spices left in which to flavor the grisly hunks of whale flesh.

"Eat up, boy. It might be a while yet before we see anything this fresh again," Jenkins huffed.

"I like the fish, though, plenty of that around here," Squid noted.

"Ha! Tell me that after you've been at sea for two or more years, with not a smidgen of green in you. God forbid the scurvy take hold of us, bleed a man from the inside out, it will."

"I don't see how the food could get much worse," said Ellison, rolling his eyes at the old whaler. "At least the fishing is good around these cursed islands."

"Watch it now, boy. That's my homeland you're speaking about," Antonio said.

Cabral smiled, elbowing Antonio. "Cursed indeed, to have spawned the likes of you."

"And you should know better than anyone, these waters be truly cursed," croaked Jenkins. "Monsters and ghost ships. Have any of us seen the like? Old Lazarus will have us all for a meal if we're not careful."

"Be quiet, old woman!" Cabral barked.

"THERE SHE BLOWS!" a voice shrieked from the crow's nest.

The crew rushed out on deck and Squid stared out the stern. Tall, shiny, black fins—a pod of whales—cut through the waves. A larger whale, just ahead of the excited pod, blew two jets of water into the air and slapped the water hard with its tale. The tall fins of the pod were circling, driving the bigger animal forward.

"Whale killers!" Cabral gasped.

"We might be able to make off with the carcass if it doesn't sink. Once they're done, that is." Antonio shrugged.

"I want to come too," exclaimed Squid.

Antonio shook his head. "It's dangerous out there."

"Let the boy go, Tony," said Jenkins. "What's the harm? By the looks of it, those killers will be doing all the work. See, there's blood in the water already."

The large whale trumpeted, bellowing angrily, the smaller, black whales grinning and squeaking with wide, toothy mouths, taunting the beast as it thrashed at them with its tail.

"Taking children with you on the longboat now, eh Islander?" chuckled Murdock. "Best leave this work to real men. You keep losing children, I hear."

Antonio's hand curled into a fist. "You're a stupid man, Murdock! With a big mouth!"

Cabral placed a hand on Antonio's shoulder and pointed towards the watching captain. "Not now," he whispered.

"Best listen to your friend. I wouldn't want to stain the deck with your blood—someone might slip in all the excitement." Murdock laughed, thumping towards his boat with his heavy harpoon.

"Squid!" Antonio barked. "Get in the boat!"

The captain scowled at the boy, and called, "Lower away!"

The longboats slammed against the water. Squid gripped an oar and shuffled away from the harpoons piled at Antonio's feet.

"Don't worry about those, boy. It'll be the killers doing the hard part," Jack said, holding his steering oar.

Twenty minutes in and Squid thought his shoulder would pop from the force of rowing. His muscles strained with each pull on the oar. The salt water that sprayed against his face stung, and he shut his eyes tightly as he lurched against the oar.

The men weren't singing this time out. They sat gawking at the strange scene before them.

The large whale had slowed, and its bellowing seemed labored and mournful. The killers were swarming around the creature, their fins rising and diving as they tightened their churning circle.

"He's a young one, he is," said Jenkins. "Won't be long now, the chase is over I think. We're in luck. They must have been harassing the beast for hours. Nice and fat, these right whales, pure blubber. It'll float long after the killers have had their fun. Up like a cork it'll bob."

"Will the killers attack us?" Squid grimaced, his knuckles white against his oar.

"No, not these ones. We'll just hang back all the same though."

Young or old, the right whale was a hulking beast. It was round and bulbous with white markings on its throat and belly. It had strange patches of thickened skin covered in crustaceans, giving the whale a rocky appearance. Its long mouth curved upwards, almost meeting with the eyes in a strange, curling smile. It had two blowholes, water sputtering out in two directions as it exhaled.

The line of longboats bobbed calmly in the ocean, waiting for the whale to die. It gave a loud moan, like rumbling thunder, the reeking stench of its breath filling Squid's nostrils.

The whalers waited. Antonio stood up and placed his foot on the boat's bow. He stood in silence, looking out at the whale whose body was swaying in tandem with the longboat.

The killers began to hop on the right whale's back, covering its blowholes. Their black, shining bodies gleamed in the sunlight as they rolled against one another. Their mouths were open in fierce yawns, showing rows of murderous, yellowed teeth.

The flippers and tail of the right whale were mangled, with chunks of its tough skin floating like liquid pearls in the water.

"There are so many of them. What are they doing to it, Jenkins?" Squid gasped.

"Probably twenty of them or so by my count, hard to tell with all their jumping about." Jenkins laughed. "They're drowning it, boy, keeping it from breathing. They'll keep tearing at it until it tires and dies."

"Why won't it just dive and escape?"

"There's no escape from the likes of them, Squid, my lad. They're the wolves of the sea!"

The harassed whale's dark, liquid eyes peered back at the boy. Its rocky head lurched up from the water's surface, desperate for a gulp of air.

The killer whales rolled over the right whale, crowding atop its lumpy back. They called to one another happily, clicking and squeaking as they danced on the surface, rejoicing at the other whale's tortured death calls.

Eventually the right whale gave one last rumble, its massive mouth—a screen of strange, long brushes—careening open. Then its body rolled in the water, and finally it died.

Squid watched as the killers swarmed along the whale's patchy face, peeling away at its flesh. In the end they ate only the lips and tongue, snatching a morsel before diving off. Their reflective fins circled the longboats. They grinned from beneath the surface, clicking and whistling at the whalers before calmly swimming away.

The right whale bobbed and rolled languidly in the water, just as Jenkins said it would. Squid felt sorry for the animal, smiling dead, with its enormously wide mouth. Squid wondered, *Is there anything so hunted as these wondrous giants?*

His mind began to wander as he stared into the animal's cavernous wounds, the blubber dancing white in the sparkling, blue waves.

Antonio turned to look at Squid, who realized he was trembling.

"Squid. Are you alright? Do you need to head back?"

Squid shook his head no, trying to overcome the nauseous feeling growing in him.

"No, I'm fine. Just a touch of sea sickness." He smiled.

The right whale's carcass was different from that of the sperm whale's: its teeth were a series of long bristles, its blubbery underside rippling up to its lipless face.

The waters were calm and shimmering, and the breeze soft and cooling. The *Sure Profit* was a good ways away, so the whalers fastened ropes to the whale and prepared their oars.

They sang as they rowed back to the distant ship, the whale's heavy body slowly towed behind them. Sharks came, wrestling in the water as they struggled for their share of the flesh.

It took several hours to get the whale back and hoisted. Squid felt as if his arms would fall out of their sockets. He thanked God for an end to the motion.

When he jumped aboard ship the other rowers patted him on the back, all except Murdock, who eyed him with disdain.

"Good job, boy!" they praised.

"Hard rowing, isn't it, boy?" Jenkins cackled, happily. "Well, you never gave up! Good for you, lad. A strong whaler you'll be. Maybe a good harpooner too."

Antonio stood behind him grinning, his big hands resting on the boy's shoulders like a proud father.

Despite Squid's misgivings, he savored the moment, but not for long; there was still work to be done. The whale had to be peeled of its skin, and its long, bristled teeth removed. The whalers explained to Squid that the baleen, made up of these bristles, was highly valued and perfect for making buggy whips, corset stays and parasol ribs. The bristles' long, flexible qualities made them indispensable in the hungry world of fashion, so naturally they carried a handsome price. They were removed and stripped clean, then bundled, tied and stored in wooden crates.

Squid tried to make himself useful, but all the power in his arms had left him. They hung heavy, making him wince as he tried to cradle the pungent bristles for bundling.

He could still see the killers' dark fins, moving in the distance, slinking through the ocean. He thought of Jenkins' description—wolves of the sea. He thought of the Dragon and his pirate crew. Were there only predators out here? The whalers, pirates and animals, all out to kill one another? Was this an ocean of monsters?

He reached down to pick up a spade and tripped. He dragged himself up, the spade scraping along the deck as he rose.

Cabral laughed at the sight of him. "Your boy doesn't quit, Antonio, even when his muscles are turned to jelly."

Antonio chuckled and called the boy over. "It will be dark soon. Off to bed with you. I won't be far behind myself."

The right whale trumpeted in his dreams, swimming dead with its streaming ropes of white blubber floating behind. Then came the clicking, and the sound of a woman's voice. He awoke in a sweat and reached for his amulet. It was gone!

Panicked, he pulled out his pockets. Nothing. He remembered falling on deck before going down to sleep. Perhaps the amulet was still there?

He sprang to the upper ship and began searching the timbers on hands and knees. Nothing. He felt his heart squeeze and a cold sweat crawl along his neck and back. It was all that was left to him of her, the only clue he had of his life before this strange ship.

His eyes moistened and his lip began trembling.

"Looking for something?" said a deep voice behind him.

It was Murdock, shoving past him with a smug expression. He was twirling the amulet around his thick, dirty fingers. The gold chain hung tightly around his hairy neck, twinkling in the morning glow.

"That's mine. Give it back!" Squid howled.

"This old thing," Murdock snorted. "'Twas a nice enough gift from my old gran," he said, inspecting it gingerly. "I think I'll keep it."

"Give it here!" Squid said, stretching out his hand.

"I don't think so," growled Murdock.

Squid lunged, clawing over the hairy giant.

Murdock seized him by the collar and threw him roughly to the floor.

"No one to protect you now, I see. Best be on your way before you get hurt. No hard feelings now, boy."

Squid screamed, jumping up and punching Murdock as hard as he could. The big whaler wasn't expecting the blow and staggered backwards.

"I'll break you in two, little fool," Murdock spat. Swinging his large fist, he slammed it against the boy's head.

Squid fell backwards, hitting the ground. Blood was trickling down his face. His lip was cracked open and bleeding, already swelling with each throb.

Hearing footsteps behind him, Squid reeled to see Antonio and Jenkins staring down at him.

"Murdock!" Antonio raged.

Jenkins hauled Squid up. "Best stay away now, lad."

"He has my medallion!" Squid yelled, head pounding.

Even in his fog, Squid could see Antonio's nostrils flaring, his face glowing red with rage.

Murdock grinned back, mocking him with the medallion. "Mine," he growled through gritted teeth.

Antonio's fist fell with a loud crack and Murdock's head jerked back violently.

Other crewmen ran up, Cabral pushing ahead of them with his harpoon.

"Let them finish it!" Jenkins hissed, holding Squid up, his lip hanging purple.

Murdock suddenly seized his harpoon and roared. His nose was gushing red, his beard smeared bloody, as he lunged for Antonio.

"I'll kill you!" he cried and swung wide. The sharpened point caught the islander's shirt, ripping it open.

As Murdock swung for another lunge, Antonio hit him hard in the chin. The giant keeled backwards, falling to the ground with a loud thud, the harpoon crashing beside him.

Cabral shoved passed Jenkins and pointed his own harpoon

at Murdock's throat.

Murdock's mouth went slack, blood seeping out of his thick, parted lips. Antonio had broken his jaw. He lay stunned, moaning and staring up in a complete stupor. He shuddered and his eyes rolled back into his shaggy head.

Antonio walked over to the sprawled giant and snatched the medallion from his burly neck. Handing it back to Squid, he gave the boy a friendly pat on the back.

"Alright?" Antonio barked, inspecting the boy's swollen lip.

"Just fine. Thank you," Squid grimaced, wiping away the blood from his forehead.

Tom waddled by and knelt next to the wounded harpooner. "Bring me my instruments."

Ellison dashed past the grumbling crowd of whalers.

Antonio took the boy's hand and climbed down to steerage. Cabral grunted at Jenkins and the two followed the harpooner below.

"Get back to work!" Squid heard Jack shout from up on deck. Then, more quietly, "What the hell happened to him?"

LEVIATHAN

"I won't condone fighting on my ship!" Stringer cried.

"It was that animal Murdock who started it, Captain. He stole, and then attacked the boy when he confronted him," Antonio said, nodding in deference to the plump little captain.

"I told you this ship is no nursery! Now one of my harpooners lies useless in the kitchens. If Tom doesn't end up killing him, it'll be a miracle, the incompetent! Murdock's face has grown to twice its size. He lies moaning and broken with a fever, a pathetic sight. I should have you whipped!" Stringer thundered.

"And who would land you your whale, my captain?" Antonio countered.

"There's more than one harpooner on this ship!" cursed Stringer.

"Not like me." Antonio straightened himself up, boldly looking the captain in the eye. Jack shook his head and swore under his breath.

Squid kept his eyes focused on the floorboards, curling his cap tight in his hands. He had no fear of the portly captain. Squid could sense that Stringer needed Antonio far more than he let on.

"I'll fine you then."

Antonio nodded curtly. "Look at the boy, Captain," Antonio implored. "Should I have let the oaf so abuse him? Murdock's been stealing and throwing his weight around since boarding in Bedford. It was bound to happen with someone eventually, my captain."

Stringer sat back. Squid found the courage to return the captain's dead stare. Even though Murdock deserved it, Squid was sure Stringer blamed him for the fight.

"Maybe, but Murdock was for me to deal with," the captain growled. "And what do we do now when we meet the big whale? Will you bring him down on your own, Islander?"

Antonio shrugged. "If I have to."

"Captain," Jack interrupted. "Surely you don't intend to …"

"I do indeed, Mr. Sillings. We keep sailing the Azores until

Lazarus fills our barrels, then we provision on São Miguel and head for home. In a few months I expect to be back in my loving wife's arms." Stinger gestured to the creepy painting behind him.

Squid made a face, forgetting to hide his disgust. Stringer's eyes narrowed on him. "I see your time with Tony here has made you a rude and petulant boy."

Antonio clenched his jaw. "Is that all, my captain?"

"No, the boy will join the rest of the crew in the forecastle."

"Like hell," Antonio grumbled.

Stringer's face went from red to purple. "You dare! I am your captain!"

"Whip me, then!" Antonio roared, slamming his fist hard against the table. The painting shook and moved off center.

"That's enough now," Jack said, placing himself between them. "The men are uneasy, Captain. Have you not seen the ships sailing away? Every merchant and shipping vessel is staying well clear of these islands. We should do the same."

Stringer leaned forward on his desk. "We go nowhere. No port until I have that whale. You promised me, Azorean. Did you not? Bring me that whale or your share is forfeit."

Antonio bowed, took the boy's hand and stormed out, slamming the door behind him.

"He's the captain, Antonio!" Cabral grumbled. "You can't speak to him like that."

"The hell I can't, the fat fool! If he'd fixed Murdock sooner none of this would have happened!" Antonio barked.

"Murdock deserved what he got," Squid mumbled, almost to himself.

Antonio glared angrily at the boy. "Is that what you think? He lies bandaged below deck now, near death most likely. Is that a good thing?"

Squid looked up at Antonio, confused and a little stunned.

The next week saw the air grow still and hot. Sluggishly, the ship dragged along with the tides until reaching the island of Terceira, the captain seeming reluctant as they weighed anchor off its shores.

Pillars of land rock spiraled to the sky off the coast, pieces of the island, cut off from the rest of the land by the ocean's endless flow.

Fishermen paddled towards the ship, babbling in their rough Portuguese with the crew. Their blue and red striped boats were sleek, rocking leisurely alongside the ship. They cast out their nets gracefully, singing long into the hot day, the ship still next to them in the gleaming water.

Antonio told Squid that the fishermen spoke of a great sea battle, mighty ships firing at one another with huge cannons. A wreck of a frigate lay broken against the rocks, waves lapping at its splintered hull and broken masts.

Squid recognized an English word in all the Portuguese chatter—Dragon—and noticed the captain looking nervously over the island's high, curving coast when he heard it too.

"Too late," Squid heard Jenkins grunt. "Now we wait for wind, and pray it takes us before some beast or devil. Nothing for it now but to sit here."

Antonio shrugged, grabbing Squid roughly by the hand. "Come on. Time for a holiday."

They rowed a longboat towards the black pebble beach, mossy green foliage leading up to tree-dense hillsides.

Antonio threw off his shirt and cap. "Time for a swim!" He grinned.

The water was cool and clear as they dove through the maze of sharp rock and coral. Live things crawled through the glowing murk, pulsing in the shimmering blue. Spiny creatures moved ponderously in and out of a thousand miniature caverns, their strange bodies swaying with the ocean's rolling. A blaze of color, soft and luminous, carpeted the sea floor and little silvery fish darted everywhere around the boy as he swam.

An octopus clung to the rock, its shapeless body bubbling out of its hole. An eye expanded from the thing's formless head—then recoiled at the boy's touch.

A pale blue shark slunk above them in the light. Antonio waved and Squid followed through a yawning green chasm.

They emerged in a salty, round pool carved out from the shoreline by the rumbling waves. The water cascaded gently over them, snaking through the island's labyrinth of black rocks.

Two girls sat washing their feet in the turquoise stillness, smiling, with blue eyes and silky, black hair.

Antonio gave them a wide grin. Covering their faces with their shawls, they ran giggling up to the hillsides.

They sat amongst the surf for a while, the sounds of now familiar church bells and whistling birds above them.

"What's this island like, Tony?" asked Squid, staring over the tall, green trees.

"Many farms and cattle … lots of green, green for miles and miles, and many rivers. A beautiful place."

"A good place to live?" asked Squid, smiling.

Antonio beamed, placing a big arm around the boy's shoulders. "Yes, a very nice place to live."

The wind picked up, grey clouds began expanding out of the golden distance.

"You're not still mad at me?" asked Squid, sheepishly. "Are you, Tony?"

Antonio burst out laughing. "No! You're a good boy. I can't blame you for being mad at Murdock, just remember … being a good man means treating everyone the way you would want to be treated, even the ones who don't deserve it. Never wish death on a person, boy. It's a great sin."

He clapped the boy on the back and dove headlong into the water. Squid took a last look at the now swaying trees and leapt after.

The ship had made good time after the squall, heading out into open water. The captain turned contemptuously from Terceira, and locked himself up in his quarters.

There'd been no sign of the great whale, and the talk of piracy had clearly unnerved him.

"It will be a long while yet before that fool can return home, rich and plump to his homely bride," Jenkins cackled.

Tom had set Murdock's jaw and the giant would soon recover enough to rejoin the crew, or so Jenkins had told Squid.

"Too bad," Squid groaned.

"Ha! Too true." Jenkins laughed.

Antonio said nothing, choosing to quietly sharpen his harpoons alongside Cabral. Tony told Squid later that he had been preoccupied with his devil whale, still hoping to land Lazarus.

"Fate will bring me to him. He's close; I feel it," he whispered to Squid from his berth that night.

The next morning was dull and gloomy, clouds wrestling colorlessly overhead. The chopping waves battered against the hull.

Squid had risen early. The strange dreams still bothered him and Antonio's snoring seemed to rattle the whole damn ship. He clutched at his medallion and stroked the scarred side of his head. Why couldn't he remember?

There were only a few crewmen on deck, still feeding the black, smoking tryworks. Squid wondered when he might finally get off this bloody ship for good. He was desperate for land, sick of the constant swaying beneath his feet. He needed solid footing. Perhaps there was a family out there waiting for him, an uncle or kindly aunt? Maybe there was still a life for him … somewhere. *Maybe it's green and pretty like Tony's Azores,* he thought.

Squid looked up at Carlos, who was snoring at the lookout.

Just the idea of land prompted Squid to leap up the riggings for a better view, as if perhaps he could will it to appear. The waves were rolling and foaming in the choppy sea. A storm was gathering, lightning crackling in the iron sky.

A large flock of angry gulls hovered below the blackening clouds, squawking over a grey lump rising ponderously in the sea. It came straight up out of the waves, a gush of water frothing atop its square head.

"THERE SHE BLOWS!" Squid shouted, scarcely thinking before forming the words.

The ship's crew scrambled below him, the captain scurrying out of his cabin. A long, white scar was plainly visible on the creature's side as it jumped up out of the water, startling the whirling gulls.

"It's him! Old Lazarus!" Jenkins hissed to the wind.

"To the boats with you! Hold fast, bury your fears and ready for the fight!" Jack shouted.

Stringer stared up at the boy, smiling at him for the first time. "Good boy! Lucky boy!"

Antonio rubbed his eyes, looking out at the whale.

Cabral stood behind him, grim-faced and ready. "Now we kill it, or it kills us, Azorean. Just what you prayed for."

Antonio turned to Squid before running for the boats. "Hold tight. Whatever happens hold on and don't worry over Antonio." He flashed the boy a toothy grin and waved goodbye.

Did Tony's own father wave to him like that, before going out to sea for the last time? Squid wondered sadly.

"Farewell, boy!" Jenkins called, not bothering to look up.

"Lower away!" yelled the captain, rubbing his fat hands together.

The longboats lined up in front of the ship, the crewmen rowing hard towards the beast.

The winds were strong and the ship kept pace. Even now the whalers sang, their voices loud and lusty as they rowed for the monster.

Lazarus dove, rising a few yards from the longboats. The monstrous whale bobbed along the frothing waves, waiting.

The air filled with the whale's eerie noises: creaking and ticking, set to its own strange rhythms. Its now familiar dull flesh was speckled white with scars, and the dangling ropes from a dozen harpoons slithered in the water around it.

Lazarus sank below the rocking boats and rose not far behind them, snorting from its blowhole, tail pointing upwards.

"Stand up!" shouted Jack, his voice trembling and hoarse.

Squid stared down from the riggings at the harpoons, held up and ready for the strike.

An enormous shadow grew beneath the ship and Squid felt a hard jolt. "Hold fast!" someone yelled below him. "He's ramming the ship!"

The *Sure Profit* began violently listing to one side. Squid could see the waves coming closer. There came another lurching jolt and the ship spun as it began righting itself.

"We're taking on water!" yelled a mate.

Squid stared at the frozen captain, who was gawking in disbelief.

The whale's body writhed in the water, circling the ship. Crewmen in the longboats grabbed harpoons and spears, throwing them at the beast in a wild panic.

"Straight to him! Bring me to him!" Antonio roared somewhere off his boat's bow.

The longboats were still in the chase.

The whale suddenly erupted out of the water, sending longboats crashing into the air.

Another harpoon flew at the whale as Cabral's boat came up close. The whale thrashed its tail, sending Cabral's men overboard. The big African fell backwards reaching for his harpoon, sprawling on his back.

The air filled with the whale's foul breath; Squid fought the urge to vomit.

"There he is again! Stab the beast! Kill it, boys!" Jack yelled.

Antonio let fly a harpoon directly into the center of the whale's square face. The iron shaft sank deep and the whale's blood flowed thick in the water.

Antonio threw another harpoon into the sinking whale, which was spewing foam from its puckered blowhole.

The whale came up and jerked its mighty head. Antonio's boat exploded in pieces, sending the whalers flying into the sea.

Ellison floated on the surface, unconscious. Jenkins reached out, too late to grab him.

"Tony!" Squid shouted. The boy could make out the harpooner's head and cap bobbing in the water as the whale swam past. Opening its long, jagged jaw the beast swallowed several of the poor whalers flailing in the water.

A horrible gurgling sound came up from Lazuras. Jack was spewing his last breath, trapped within the whale's grinding jaws. The first mate was still gripping his steering oar, eyes bulging in agony.

Antonio yelled something threatening at the whale in Portuguese. He made to stab the whale with his remaining harpoon, the wake from the monster's tail sending him rolling back into the sea.

Squid felt the salty spray of the waves slapping against his face. The ship was sinking beneath him, falling into the water on its side, the whale's creaking call mixing with the sounds of the splintering ship. The gulls had begun hovering above him, watching the vessel break apart.

The boy climbed up as high as he could, wrapping his arms around the thick ropes. A body floated past him, a white apron rippling in the water. Tom's lazy eye peered up at him, dead and frozen.

Captain Stringer was still holding onto his doomed ship, clutching the sinking mainmast.

The men screamed as Lazarus attacked the remaining longboats, crashing with his full weight on top of them.

A figure began clawing up towards Squid, face swollen and bandaged. Murdock's hairy hands were grasping for any sort of leverage to draw him up.

Squid untangled one of his arms and reached for the big man. With a crack the ropes began to break and Murdock's bandaged face sank into the murky blue.

The reeling ship spun, Squid's stomach lurching with the ship's final groan.

The ocean frothed all around him, broken masts and riggings a tangled mass. Squid released his grip on the sinking ship, but its pull was irresistible. He was going down with it.

The water was dark and cold. Squid felt his breath catch as he sank. He felt his body tense, his movements clumsy as he struggled for the surface. The ship's wake was sucking him down. Bodies were floating everywhere around him, sinking deeper into the ocean's murky blackness. In a panic he gasped, the salty water filling his lungs.

He kicked with all his might towards the surface light above, the whale's monstrous shadow passing below him.

He felt a tug on his leg and fought back against the whale's drag. His leg had a knotted old rope wrapped around it. It was from one of the harpoons, still attached to the sinking beast.

The surface was getting farther and farther away. A burning pain gripped his chest and his arms flailed in panic.

The ticking rippled through the black ocean, the leviathan pausing, hovering for a moment.

Lazarus turned, staring up at the boy, before slowly moving on him.

Looking up, Squid saw the outline of a man diving down from the surface. Antonio was swimming as hard as he could, his hand out, fingers extended.

Reaching under Squid's legs, he untangled the rope. The outline of a single longboat passed overhead. Antonio tugged on the boy's arm, kicking up to the light.

The whale slunk under, its head nudging the whaler's feet. Squid turned to glare at the creature's crooked and hanging jaw.

The leviathan groaned, studying the child, its square head close to Squid. Then it curled its wrinkled back, melting into the darkness from which it came, the bodies of the ship's crew sinking after it.

Squid was then hauled up into the light, heaving and coughing the salty water from his tired lungs.

"Get it all out, boy," Antonio gasped.

Hands pawed at them. Squid found himself on Cabral's longboat. The side of the African's head was bleeding and his hand was cut. Jenkins lay gasping beside him. Carlos was weeping at the stern, his long, black hair draped low over his forehead. Squid looked around at the wind-swept sea, he and the four whalers—the only survivors.

"They're gone," Cabral hissed. "The whole ship is down and gone. We're all that's left."

"What now?" Carlos shouted.

Antonio wheezed, then pointed towards the grey horizon and the distant Azores. "We go home."

THE FOG

The storm had churned the sea into one massive swirl, the longboat rolling ponderously over mountainous waves. The thunder rumbled overhead, and lightning crackled all around them, blazing in the rumbling sky. The wind and rain cut into their worn faces. A wet chill soaked deep into the bones of the four weary survivors, and Squid began shaking uncontrollably.

The tempest ended as suddenly as it began, the longboat lolling gently in the water. Squid looked up. Antonio's home seemed a little closer, a hazy smudge growing out from the sea.

As they rowed, heaving their shoulders against broken oars, a mist set in, a descending white fog that clouded everything in a smoky soup.

"We don't have much water. The sooner we get to that island the better," said Jenkins.

Squid was growing paler with each shiver, his teeth rattling in his skull.

"Don't worry. We'll be home soon," Antonio soothed, pointing at the rocky silhouette rising before them. *"Nossa ilha,* São Miguel. My island is close."

"Where did this infernal mist come from?" Jenkins grumbled. "Monsters and fog so thick you can barely see the front of your own nose. Lovely. Charming place, your island."

"Shut up, old man!" Cabral growled.

Reflective shapes swam past the longboat, squeaking and whistling as they elegantly cut through the water. One of the creatures jumped, splashing the men with its tail. A slender face popped up, smiling off the bow.

Squid gawked at the smooth, reflective creature, its black, liquid eyes shining up at him.

"Dolphins!" cried Carlos. "A good omen!"

"Annoyance, more like it," murmured Jenkins.

"No, he's right. Many a time these creatures have saved a drowning man, leading him back to my island's shores," said Antonio.

Antonio grimaced and shook his head. "How could we have

let that happen? I speared the beast right through the head. I stabbed him, damn it!"

"There's no killing that thing, Tony. I told you such," Jenkins huffed.

"You speak all kinds of nonsense. What choice did Antonio have? Any of us have? The captain wanted that whale, so we rowed for it. It's our trade. Men died, but that's the way of it. They're gone, whalers to the last. No point in dwelling on it!" Cabral barked, placing a hand on Antonio's shoulder. "Best forget it now, brother. Nothing for it."

Antonio sat with his shoulders shaking.

One of the dolphins turned towards them chattering and nodding its head. Then it propelled itself out of the water and disappeared, the rest of its pod following it into the fog.

"Huh! Dolphins," muttered Jenkins, wringing out his soaking cap.

It was hours before they heard the surf and saw black rocks forming out from the salty mist.

"I recognize this coast, at least I think I do," Antonio hissed. There was something ominous in the air, something strange about the silence.

"Where are all the ships?" Jenkins grumbled.

"Keep rowing. I know a beach nearby. Soon we'll be near my village, Luz. The old priest will take care of us. Not long now," Antonio said.

"You smell that, Cabral?" Jenkins whispered.

Cabral nodded, sniffing the air cautiously.

"No ships, just the stench of fire."

They rowed solemnly down the coast, the waves crashing over the rocks before them. The surf roared in Squid's ears and rocked the boat from side to side.

"Look," Carlos gasped, crossing himself.

A coastal village was up ahead of them, the fishing boats smoking black along the pebbly beach. The village looked deserted; a wispy-looking dog rummaged through an overturned basket. The houses were empty, ashen husks. A corpse lay smoldering on the ground as fires crackled along the forest edge.

"I know this place," Antonio growled. "What happened here?"

"Pirates," Cabral said through gritted teeth.

"There's no end to our bad luck," grumbled Jenkins.

Antonio stared about the coast. It was impossible to see anything far ahead.

"We'll continue on. I don't hear anything but waves, and the fog should cover us," Antonio said. "We'll keep going towards the village, agreed?"

They all nodded. Jenkins mumbling to himself, "Why're you asking me all a sudden? No one ever listens to old Jenkins."

"My head is killing me. Please shut up, old man," Cabral moaned.

The fog only thickened as they rowed by the forested coast.

Occasionally a grey-brown gull would fly past the boat, crashing out of the fog with its heavy wing beats.

"Who's that?" gasped Carlos.

A boy stood on a rock, his dark eyes looking out at the longboat. His clothes were torn, his face covered in soot and dried blood.

There was nowhere to land the boat, so Antonio called out to him.

"Rapaz, de onde você é. O que aconteceu aqui? Boy, where are you from? What happened here?"

The child hopped off the tall rock and dashed back into the misty forest.

"This doesn't look good, Tony," whispered Jenkins.

"Quiet. You'll frighten Squid!" Antonio hissed.

"We're all frightened!" cursed a shivering Carlos.

The whalers rowed on.

Nearing a grey, sandy beach, Squid noticed a long dock, missing boards and full of crooked planks.

"We should keep going, at least to the other side of the beach. Just to be sure it's safe," Cabral whispered.

"Agreed," Antonio nodded.

A single black fishing boat bobbed ahead of them. Squid peered over and found it empty, a broken oar stretched across its sides.

Suddenly, a man came running out of the mist towards them, out of breath and eyes wild with fear.

"*Ajuda!* Help!" he screamed with open arms.

The whalers froze, watching the man bolt into the water.

An axe swirled through the smoky white, embedding with a crunch in his back.

"*Aqui!*" Antonio yelled, rowing for him.

The man's mouth opened wide as he sank into the surf.

"No!" Cabral shouted at a leaping Antonio.

A shadow appeared on the dark sand, with hulking, square shoulders and a raised pistol. It was a huge man, covered in strange tattoos, including a large, black dragon inked across his chest. Squid noticed his bald head was covered in some kind of writing. He stood snarling through black teeth and murderous eyes.

Antonio grabbed the wounded man and tried to lift him into the longboat.

"He's dead, man! Leave him be!" yelled Jenkins.

The man's head lobbed to one side, his eyes open and lifeless.

Antonio grimaced as he let the body fall from his grip.

The tattooed man fired, the shot splintering the bow of the boat.

"Row, damn you!" Cabral shouted.

Squid reached for his oar, the man on the beach howling as they pulled away.

As they retreated down the coast, the shape of a ship peeled away from the fog, a large, three-mast vessel; rows of cannons yawned back at them.

Shots rang out, exploding in the water around the longboat.

"The beach! We'll make a run for it. Escape in the mist," Antonio spat.

The boat landed, crunching hard against the sand. Farther down the beach the large, tattooed figure was yelling, the shadows of other men forming up around him. Squid felt Cabral's massive hand pull him off his seat and they all started running. Musket fire began cracking over them.

"There should be a tree line just left of the town. We'll make for that!" Antonio rasped.

A long, stone wall rose ahead of them, dense trees and foliage growing from off its ridge. Just over the black stones and mortar lay Antonio's village, the thatchings of several roofs just visible overhead. Squid hoped that if they could get behind the walled defense, they would be safe from the pirates.

Pistols sparked in the smoky air. Carlos fell, screaming.

The whalers stooped to help him. Jenkins lifted Carlos over his shoulders.

Suddenly, men were everywhere around them, laughing behind grubby faces and red-stained axes. They wore bright red headscarves and sashes, billowing pants and shirtsleeves.

A man in black hobbled towards them, a floppy hat covering his face. His wooden leg dragged as he shuffled awkwardly through the grey sand.

Squid had the sensation of knowing him. He had seen those tattered clothes and that wide-brimmed hat before.

The strange man hurried over, carrying two pistols, his beady, black eyes shining behind a knot of scars and wrinkles.

"Scrab!" Jenkins gulped.

"You've heard of me?" The man smirked. "Good."

The tattooed giant stalked behind him, growling inside a mask of black ink.

Cabral, still holding the harpoon, pointed it at Scrab's chest.

"Let us go, or you'll be the first to die!" Antonio grunted.

"Ha!" Scrab spat. The pirate slowly moved his pistol towards Squid's head. "Not before the boy."

Antonio glared, his face growing pale. "Drop it, Cabral."

Cabral hesitated but eventually let go of his harpoon.

"Wonderful! We survived the monster whale for this! From one set of jaws to another!" Jenkins spat. "Damn your islands, Tony! Haven for monsters and rogues, I say!"

Scrab's eyes flew open and the pistol shook in his hands.

"What say you?" Scrab hissed. "What know you of a whale? Tell me, damn you! A monster, with a long, white tear stretched across it? Is that the animal you speak of?"

The pirates closed in on them, their faces suddenly tense.

The whalers stared back in confusion.

"What's wrong with your ship?" asked Squid innocently, pointing at the *Red Gull*, anchored precariously off the shoreline.

The ship was listing to one side. As the fog lifted it was plain to see she had suffered some damage, a big hole gaping in her side.

"Twice we've sailed out and it's come on us, battering at the hull with its cursed head!" Scrab yelled.

The whalers stared at one another.

Jenkins peered intently, evaluated the damage with a wincing stare. Then his head flew back and the old man started laughing, his cackle reverberating down the beach.

Scrab slammed the end of his pistol on the old man's head, sending him crashing down.

Cabral gave Scrab a shove and the old pirate careened backwards.

Jenkins howled all the louder, a red trickle running down his downy, white sideburns.

"What do you find so funny?" Scrab shouted.

"Do you ever shut up, old man?" hissed Cabral, looking down into the barrel of Scrab's pistol.

"Lazarus! The damn whale has it in for all of us," wheezed Jenkins.

Scrab lowered his pistol and gestured at the tattooed giant behind him. "Kill them, Billy!"

"Scrab!" came a booming voice from the ship. "What's going on down there?"

"Nothing, Captain! Just some whalers, sailing home for a last visit."

"Bring them to me, Mr. Scrab. Alive, please!"

Scrab trembled with rage. The old whaler just wouldn't stop laughing.

THE GREY DOGS

"How long do you expect us to stay here?" asked Lob, rubbing the hollow socket where his eye used to be.

"Until the ship's repaired and the captain says otherwise," Scrab hissed.

The fires burned high in the night, the pirates huddling around the flames in pockets all along the beach.

The smell of burning pitch hung heavy. Scrab worried there wouldn't be enough to plug the ship good and proper.

"I hope he's got a plan," said Lob. "We can't stay here all

exposed like. We got lucky off that island. Which one was it now—Terceira? Can't keep 'em all straight in my head, so different and yet the same they are to one another. If it ain't the damn whale, it'll be another ship—French, Portuguese, English … they're all looking for us out here." The fruit Lob was eating dripped in red globs down his yellow-grey beard. He was Scrab's closest thing to a friend, the only one who dared speak to him with anything close to frankness.

"He has a plan. I don't know it but he has one. Plays it cool, he does," said Scrab.

"Talbot thinks we should break for open water, soon as the ship is pitched and timbered proper again," Lob croaked.

"We've already tried that. The beast nearly took us."

"Aye, but we've been here awhile now. Maybe the captain's lost his nerve," Lob said, chewing his food loudly.

Scrab glared at Lob, his eyes narrowing on the old pirate. "Shut up! You know what will happen if he catches you saying that."

"Ha! I'm an old sea dog. I can say what I please," Lob said, staring around the fire cautiously. "It's true and you know it. Even he's been spooked by that thing. Twice we've gone out after repairs and twice it's rammed us, taking more of our men down with it. Cursed these islands be, Scrab. You feel it in your bones same as I. If we stay here, we hang or starve. If we sail, we drown, and go straight to hell or worse."

Scrab shrugged. "What do you expect me to do about it, old

fool? I tell you he has a plan."

"Talk to 'im. Tell 'im we can't wait much longer. Those damn villagers are getting to be better shots—took two of us today."

Scrab sighed. "Aye, I know it."

Scrab stared at the village wall. Everything was burnt and crumbling around it, but the wall was still standing. It was built up with the same black, volcanic rock that made up the island. Everything seemed built of the stuff out here, he mused.

The village of Luz was a simple place, with white houses lining curved, cobbled pathways. It nestled against a high cliff. A waterfall cascaded from above, pooling fresh water into reservoirs below. The cursed, black rocks framed everything in Luz too, from steps to chimneys.

At the village's center sat the church. It was painted the same white as many of the homes in the village, with a pair of large, green doors guarding the entrance. Its façade curved upwards, hugging the large, black cross at its roof.

A massive, black statue stood at the base of its steps: a great, winged angel with a sword raised up over its fierce head. It was the same protective statue as always in these parts, God's warring angel, Saint Michael, the cursed island's namesake.

"Why did he spare those whalers? For that scrawny boy maybe? Dougan's never bothered with the little ones before. What's he playing at?" Lob sighed. "We're leaving orphans up and down this damn coast. Better to kill them now. More mercy in that, I think."

"I agree. I don't like the look of those men, the boy especially.

We should have done them in," Scrab grumbled.

A dog howled from the wall, its amber eyes reflecting moonlight in the black. The islanders bred them large here, big beasts with tanned stripes running down their grey hides. Their ears and tails were cropped short, making them look more feral somehow, meaner.

"Those dogs give me the shivers," Lob hissed.

"They've killed more than a few of us." Scrab grimaced, aiming his pistol. The dog gave a loud bark and leapt down from the black stones.

The wall gave good cover. The pirates had been unable to breach it. They had charged, howled and burned everything around for miles, but the village held. The few pirates who managed to get over had either been shot outright or torn up by the dogs, their screams carrying over the stones.

They had caught a couple of runners, messengers making a break for the island's capital. Dougan had them tortured and propped their bodies up on poles along the beach for the villagers to see. They had begun to stink and rot in the hot sun. Scrab winced at the smell and spat the foul air from his throat.

Normally they would have been long gone by now—easy spoils, these islands. But the monster was waiting for them, somewhere out there. Even now Scrab thought he could hear its tortured creaking from off the water.

"We can't stay like this. We're too exposed. We need to take that village and sail forth, quick, cannons a'ready," Scrab mused.

Lob grunted in approval as Scrab rose, shuffling towards the ship.

Scrab loved the *Red Gull,* from bowsprit to rudder. He felt part of it, a living and breathing extension of its riggings, masts and sails. The men saluted as he passed. He adored and hated every one of them.

There was no homelier, no more fearsome crew in all the seas. They would do anything for him and Scrab knew it. It was Dougan however, their pirate prince, they truly loved; handsome, fearless and ruthless, the blood-stained Dragon. Scrab always limped behind, doing the difficult killing, the kind that most men didn't have the stomach for. He had severed more heads than the crew could count, not caring who or what was in his way. He was no prince, to be sure, just an old and pitiless pirate devoted to captain and ship.

He could hear the Dragon's boots, thudding along the bow as he paced. A hand rested on the pummel of his sword and a scowl was twisted over his striking face.

"You know the men aren't happy," Scrab said, shuffling up.

"What of it?" Dougan grumbled.

"The whalers?" Scrab shrugged.

"They may come in handy." Dougan grinned.

"I don't like the look of 'em, the one with the scar especially. He knocked two of the crew senseless when they were dragging him down to the hold."

Dougan chuckled. "How did that happen?"

"They pushed the boy to hurry 'im along and the whaler went mad. Took four of us to pin the brute down."

"Did you hurt him?" Dougan hissed.

"No, just as you ordered, they're safe and cozy below. The old one keeps laughing, mocking us. The crew wants his throat slit."

"Just keep them alive, for now." Dougan sighed.

They looked down on the black beach. The wind made the palms rustle. Shapes emerged from the wall, the crew lining up to meet them.

"Hold your fire!" Dougan barked.

A tall, old man, draped in black, formed out from the darkness. His white hair and beard rippled with the breeze. A shining, silver cross dangled from his chest as he walked forward with his staff. Two villagers stood behind him, the torches trembling in their hands. They looked about the pirate camp wide-eyed, hiding behind the black-robed figure.

One of the large field dogs skipped forward, sniffing anxiously at air. Its eyes flickered in the firelight before calmly sitting at the old man's feet.

The old man held up a big, veined hand. "We come in peace." His voice was deep and commanding, his expression firm and resolute. "I am Father Aldo. I have come to plead for the bodies of my countrymen and to beseech you to leave our shores."

The priest stood waiting amongst the twisted faces of the

crew as Dougan and Scrab marched through the black, sparkling sand. Scrab made sure to keep his hand firmly on his pistol, eyes narrowed on the big dog.

"Why so much concern for the dead, old priest?" asked Dougan, gesturing to the lifeless husks above them. In the darkness they barely seemed human, swaying with the island's tall trees.

"We want to give these men a proper burial. It is our duty," the priest answered calmly.

Dougan smiled at the old man. "You have courage. I like that. Open your village to me! Let my men take a few spoils from your church and we can end this unpleasantness. Or better yet, make a generous payment for the bodies of your brave men, a tribute so we can depart as friends."

The crew chuckled, Lob's cackling pitching higher than the rest.

The priest bowed and kneeled before the pirate captain, the laughter ceasing as Dougan's face froze into a frown.

"We are poor. This is a simple fishing village with little to offer except what the island can grow. We are God's children and we beg of you mercy."

The men grumbled and shifted awkwardly amongst themselves. Scrab hobbled up and hissed in the captain's ear, "Send him away, or kill him. Sacred old men can only bring us trouble. Our men are spooked enough without this display!"

Talbot waddled behind, stroking his red beard and grimacing.

"Bad luck to kill a priest, Captain. We've skewered enough of 'em in our day to be sure, but the men be more than a little on edge. Too much bad luck of late, too much."

Dougan glared at Talbot and bared his teeth. Talbot took a step back and lowered his eyes, demurely removing his tricorne hat.

The Dragon exhaled a long breath and looked down at priest contemptuously. "Take the bodies and go home, old man."

Father Aldo looked up. "Bless you, my son," he said, giving the captain a solemn nod.

Big Billy pushed his way past the crowd and glared at Scrab. His face twisted in a scowl before spitting on the ground.

"Cut them down!" yelled Dougan, unsheathing his sword from its scabbard. "Now! Before I cut you in two!"

Big Billy gulped and ran up the beach.

The crew watched as Billy took down and carried the bodies, pale and rotting, over to the priest. He dropped them with an unceremonious thud, the big dog yelping at the stench.

The Azoreans dragged the bodies to their village, and with a final nod, the priest melted silently back into the darkness.

"Too much bad luck is right," Lob muttered at Scrab's side.

"I know," grumbled Scrab.

He watched the captain march back to his ship, before turning to stare at the moonlit sea crashing against the cursed, black rocks. Scrab cocked his ear and listened for the whale's creaking. Nothing.

The man shuffled away quietly. Only the sounds of surf and sand remained, crunching beneath his wooden leg.

THE HOLD

There were strange noises in the stinking darkness, hammers rapping against the hull, footsteps and howls. Something was braying nearby, its tiny hooves scraping against the floorboards.

The smell was nauseating, sickly sweet. Sometimes the stink from the pitch would seep through the timbers, making Squid wretch. The floor was slick, covered in black grime. He was chained to the wall, just outside of the whalers' cage.

The fat pirate with the red beard had come down, peering at the whalers in the light of his lantern, through the bars of their cell. "No more trouble! Best lie there and wait for what the captain has planned for ya. Can't be too bad, otherwise he would have killed you by now."

Jenkins spat at him through the bars. The fat man cursed and grumbled back up the dark stairs.

Enough light entered through the hold's crooked door for Squid to see a goat, limping along the black floor. Barrels and crates littered the ground, rotting food hung from the ceiling and caked the corners of the black hold. Rats peeked out of corners, squeaking and arguing in the darkness.

His hands were clasped in iron, the metal biting into his wrists.

"Squid!" Antonio whispered. "Are you alright, boy?"

"I'm fine, Tony. But they have me in irons."

"Aye," groaned Jenkins. "Such is our fate, trapped in this filthy ship."

"Why would they separate us?" growled Antonio.

"To torment you," said Cabral. "You gave them a good licking!"

Antonio groaned, stroking the swollen side of his face. "They took the boots to me. My head's ringing."

"What do they have planned for us?" Carlos whimpered, his wounded leg stretched out on the floor, the bandages seeping red.

"Rest up," Antonio whispered. "Try not to move too much."

"We have to get the lad out of here, Tony," Cabral whispered.

"He's lost a lot of blood—the wound is already festering in this heat."

Antonio growled and shook the bars. "Hey! Hey! Get down here! My friend is hurt! He needs help!" he hollered at the top of his lungs.

"Save your breath, Tony," Jenkins moaned. "They don't care."

Squid sat in the darkness for a moment, the sound of Carlos' tortured breathing rasping in his ears. He thought of the woman in his dreams, his mother, the whale and everyone on the *Sure Profit,* all rotting in the sea. It made him angry, a feeling of rage boiling inside him. He was past fear of dying, past pain and past weariness. All he wanted now was to make sense of it all—his visions, the holes in his memory. His life seemed to him, at that moment, profoundly unfair.

The rage grew and grew as he began tugging on the iron clasp, shaking the heavy chains.

"Squid," Antonio growled. "What are you doing? You'll hurt yourself, boy!"

Squid felt the skin on his palms tear, his blood dribbling on his boots.

"Squid! Stop it!"

The chain rattled and clanked, echoing in the cavernous hold. The goat limped past him, curious at the noise. Its leg was swollen and it bleated meekly with eyes half-closed.

Squid winced with the pain, but he felt the iron clasp slowly slipping from his hands. Then he gave a violent jerk, the top layer of skin peeling off his folded fingers and palms. The irons fell with a loud clank, the little goat scurrying away.

"Good lad!" Jenkins cackled.

"These chains weren't made for children!" Squid grimaced, a chunk of skin hanging from his left hand.

Antonio ripped a strip from his coat. "Here, wrap this around it. Wash the wound clean, soon as you're off ship."

Flakes of rust covered Squid's arms and fingers, the stinging pain rippling through him, stoking his anger. "I'm not going anywhere without you!"

"With any luck the mist is still with us. The hammering's stopped and I don't hear anything above us. Most of them are probably on the beach. Sneak up and over the ship. Swim if you have to. Just get away, away from the village if you can!" Antonio whispered.

"I won't," Squid hissed.

"The old one with one eye has the keys," Jenkins croaked from behind the bars. "I saw them on him after they locked us up. He's a ripe old drunk. I smelled it on him. He'll probably be at that bottle I saw him carrying. Sneak them off him, lad!"

"Jenkins!" Antonio growled.

"The boy can do it. He's a brave and capable lad. Let him try, Tony!"

Squid couldn't see Antonio's expression in the shadows, but he could hear the torment in his voice as he protested.

"I'll be back!" Squid whispered, gingerly climbing the dark, filthy stairs.

A shaft of ghostly light glowed through the trapdoor. The door creaked as Squid carefully peeked out—the old, one-eyed pirate's deep snores rumbling from the other side. The pirate was sitting with a jug in his lap, hunched over with his rump pressed against the door. A lantern lay next to him, illuminating the mid-deck and stairs leading to the upper part of the ship.

Squid gave the door a shove and the old pirate toppled over, his remaining eye half-open as he drooled on the deck.

The keys were tied to his belt, inches from Squid's face.

Squid stared hard at the light peering in from the upper part of the ship; it seemed murky and dull … perhaps the fog was still heavy?

Squid quickly shut the door at the sound of laughter approaching. He waited a moment for the footsteps to march away.

Squid gently opened the door again with his shoulder, the hinges creaking. He stretched out his hand. His arm was just small enough to get through the opening, still obstructed by the old pirate snoring on the floor above. His fingers just reached the ring on the pirate's belt. Curling his fingers around the keys, he ripped them off the pirate's tattered pants. The door slammed harder than he intended and the keys jingled. The withered belt had ripped off with the keys, and the buckle rang loudly as it fell to the floor below him. He cocked his ear to the door; the pirate's snoring was still audible from the other side.

"Good lad!" Jenkins beamed as Squid struggled with the keys.

After several tries the bars swung open and Antonio lifted him in a big bear hug. "Brave boy!" he chuckled.

The little goat trembled, nuzzling up to the boy as the whalers made for the opening. Antonio shooed the thing away. Pushing up against the door, Antonio gently lifted and shoved the old pirate out of the way. The others clamored up after him.

Squid paused a moment, staring at the quivering goat, feeling sorry for it.

"Come on!" Cabral hissed. "Leave the thing."

The pirate was face down. His jug of wine had spilled everywhere, over and around him.

A big figure turned towards them as they entered the mid-deck.

"You!" the red-bearded pirate blurted, before the blow silenced him.

Cabral had knocked him to the ground beside the older pirate, a pair of the big man's gold teeth coming loose and rattling across the deck.

Jenkins stuffed the big man back down the hold quickly and quietly, grabbing the sword from his portly waist and holding it close to his side. The whalers made their way through the black insides of the ship without seeing anyone else. Same luck as they reached the upper deck, grateful the ship was strangely empty. They hurried to the main deck. Antonio carried Carlos over his shoulder.

The cockboat was hanging empty, roped tight to the hull. It was larger than the other boats, presumably to ferry supplies from shore to ship.

"Get in!" Antonio whispered. "If we're lucky no one will notice us in the mist, or they'll think it's just another resupply. We won't get far in this thing over water, too slow, but if we hurry on foot along the side of the beach we can make the trees and get into the village."

They rowed quietly towards the shore, ready to make a run for the village, the fires from the pirate camp glowing in the fog.

"Stop them! Stop them! You fools!" The pirate dressed all in black—Squid remembered his name was Scrab—yelled in a hoarse voice from the ship above them.

The whalers began rowing as hard as they could, the pirates running towards them on the beach.

The boat landed before the pirates could reach them.

Antonio leapt off, screaming something at Cabral in Portuguese. The African shook his head but Antonio pushed off, running down the beach, towards the wall and sheltering forest of trees.

Antonio gripped his oar, swinging it at the advancing pirates. Two pirates fell at his feet, their swords tumbling from their hands.

Cabral grabbed Squid and made a dash for the tree line.

"Antonio!" Squid yelled. "No, we can't leave him!"

Jenkins and Carlos were running behind them, Carlos

dragging his broken leg. An axe swirled through the fog, catching the young whaler in the back. He whirled and fell dead against the sand.

"No! Damn you! The captain wants them alive!" yelled Scrab.

Antonio growled and jabbed his broken oar into a pirate's chest. The man screamed, crumbling into the surf.

Several men were circling him now, Antonio swinging at them with his fists.

Squid felt his legs leave the ground as Cabral began dragging him away.

He saw Jenkins kneeling over Carlos' body, the old man unsheathing the sword he'd taken from the big pirate from his side. Jenkins gave Squid a little nod, before running back towards Antonio.

The pirates were swarming over Antonio, Jenkins swinging wildly at them with his blade.

The big tattooed one, Billy, pushed past, knocking the sword contemptuously from Jenkins' hands.

Antonio was pinned to the ground, Jenkins gasping beside him. Billy kicked Jenkins down, raising a curved saber.

The last thing Squid saw before being enveloped in the forest green was Jenkins' old head, rolling on the ground.

Antonio roared, his cries echoing through the trees.

THE PRIEST

S quid couldn't breathe. Cabral's hand was clasped tight against his face.

"Quiet, boy. They'll hear us!"

The African's eyes were bloodshot and his hand was shaking. His black face was beaded with heavy drops of sweat.

"Damn that old man!" he hissed, his voice strained with emotion. "Don't move!"

The pirates were hacking through the forest, twigs and bamboo snapping beneath their boots.

Squid's heart was racing, the taste of bile rising in his throat.

Cabral hastily piled up some foliage in an effort to blend with the forest growth, lying flat and still, holding Squid tight in his arms.

"I saw them go through here!" one of the men yelled, chopping down a small tree with his saber.

"They couldn't have just vanished!" said another.

"We should get back. We're too close to the wall."

Squid shut his eyes, balling his wounded hand into a tight fist. He shrunk under Cabral's arms, trying not to shake in terror. He could still see Jenkins' grimaced expression in his mind's eye.

"That big whaler's a tough one," said one of the voices.

"Aye, that old one gave as good as he got, too. Billy took right good care of him, same as he always does."

"What about the captain? How do we tell him we lost the other two?"

"Scrab will soothe 'im. It's a bad idea, keeping men like that about. We should have killed 'em when we first had the chance."

"What do you think the captain's thinking?"

"I don't know, but we best pray he's in a good mood when we see 'im next."

A musket shot rang out from the wall, a ball of puffy, white smoke escaping into the air.

"Get back! We're too few and they're gone anyway!" a pirate shouted, running for the clearing.

Cabral called out desperately to the villagers behind the wall in Portuguese.

Squid listened to the musket balls whizzing through the palms. Cabral's heavy breath was hot in his ear. The pirates were gone. Cabral kept his grip on Squid's mouth, laying still for a long while, as they waited for the musket fire to subside. Light peeked through the blown-out canopy and everything grew silent, Cabral finally releasing his grip.

Squid popped his head up to hear a clamor of voices and barking. A big fellow with a thick beard poked his head over the rocks, his musket aimed at Cabral's head.

Cabral raised his arms and called out in Portuguese again to the man.

The man waved his hand, beckoning them closer.

The wall was made up of large stones grown mossy and slippery. Squid slipped and Cabral hoisted him over.

Several enormous dogs were barking as he climbed down, grey and menacing. The Azoreans held the beasts back by their collars and held their muskets aimed squarely at Cabral.

Cabral collapsed on the ground and wiped the sweat from his face. Men ran up to them, stocky-looking fellows carrying workmen's axes and pistols. A hand held out a clay cup. Squid snatched it, gulping down the water.

Cabral began speaking and gesturing in a flurry of Portuguese. Squid strained to listen, but couldn't understand any of it.

The Azoreans gawked at the boy. A short, Azorean man with

a long, red cap stooped down to examine Squid's wounded hand. He quickly cleaned the scrapes, applying a foul-smelling alcohol and slimy, green plant secretion. Squid winced and held his breath with the sudden pain. Then the man pulled out a needle and thread, running the needle through him to sew the wound up tight. The pain was excruciating, and Squid struggled to stay still. Cabral grabbed the boy's hand and held it for the needle. Squid felt fresh tears well up in his eyes, but he fought them back, focusing his thoughts on Antonio.

One of the big dogs came out from behind the little man and began licking Squid's face. A few of the Azoreans began to laugh.

"Forgive them. They have never seen the dogs behave so meekly with a stranger," said a voice from the parting crowd of men. "They like you, it seems. It's a good omen."

The old man who had spoken leaned in, a heavy cross glittering against his dark robes. A kind smile spread from under his long whiskers.

"I am Father Aldo. Welcome to the village of Luz."

Cabral sprung up and bowed to the old man reverently. More Portuguese quickly tumbled out of him as the crowd of villagers expanded.

Aldo was almost the same height as Cabral and just as imposing. The two seemed easy in each other's company.

"I know your protector quite well, young man," Father Aldo said to Squid, bowing. "A good man, a very good man indeed."

"You have to go out there! You must do something! They'll kill him!" Squid shouted.

Father Aldo placed a hand on Squid's shoulder. "I know what you are feeling, my son, but be patient."

"Be patient?" Squid shrieked. "How can you say that? You can't just leave him out there! You said you knew him, that he was a good man. He's one of you!"

The crowd began to solemnly disperse, many shaking their heads sadly.

"Squid, listen to the father," said Cabral, eye level with him. "These people are too few. If not for the wall this village would have been burned with the rest. They've lost many men."

"I'm afraid that's true," sighed Father Aldo. "Look around you, my son. We have all lost someone we care about these last few days."

Feeling helpless, Squid let his attention turn outward and stared at the passing villagers. They were sullen, weary and bone-tired. Some of the women were wearing black; they stared with ghostly expressions through knitted veils. Others had colorful, wide skirts, and wore headscarves or straw hats, hair running down their backs in raven-colored waves.

Most of the men wore heavy boots, some simple, wooden shoes. A few were barefoot, with an axe or spade hanging heavy at their side. Their clothes were worn, but clean and well looked after. They also wore peculiar caps, dark in color and made of a thick fabric with a short cape running out the back, covering their necks and shoulders. They had a grim, prideful look that seemed to defy their circumstances.

"Surely there's something we can do for Tony." Squid turned his attention back to the priest.

"Fear not. We can pray. They are keeping him for some purpose. Otherwise why spare him?" Aldo soothed. "Come with me, my boy, so we may talk more privately."

Cabral stayed back, leaning against the wall. An Azorean walked up, grinned broadly and handed him a musket.

"You have lived some time with these men, these whalers?" Aldo asked as they climbed the cobbled path.

"They're my friends, or rather, were my friends. So many of them are gone."

The village was quite simple and pleasant, following the natural contours of the rich, green landscape. The pathways wound upwards towards the base of the cliff. White houses and stone cottages seemed crammed together, bright green shutters decorating the entranceways.

Three women stood speaking in front of an especially large home. The stone foundation of the house was covered in moss. There was a colorful bird chatting in a cage by an open window.

To Squid the women seemed very oddly dressed, in long blue-black robes, covering all but their ankles. The hoods of their capes were enormous, billowing out at least a foot in front of them, obscuring their young faces like enveloping tents. They gave Aldo demurring nods as he walked on, and he blessed them with a quick gesture as he passed.

Squid stared after them, not knowing what to make of their garments.

"The hoods are edged with whale bone to keep their shape. It is an old fashion here on our island. You will get used to the sight of them, I hope."

One of the women smiled at Squid as he looked back at them. He waved timidly.

Gardens were everywhere, vines and flowers clinging to every wall and gateway. Dogs—skinny, tanned creatures with long, curled tails—ran about the streets with nervous eyes.

A heard of sheep jumbled by, bleating and prancing. A man on a donkey forced them along with a long stretch of bamboo.

Fruits and greens grew everywhere, their aromas mixing with the smell of fresh bread that wafted from open windows.

Squid could hear the waterfall rumbling behind the village. He felt the damp air caress his cheeks. Children were gathering, laughing and playing as their parents drew out the water. The many boys and girls seemed to be running free, some of them quite young and barely out of swaddling, their grubby faces smiling as they pointed at Squid.

Squid was bewildered. A feeling of relief crept up on him. He felt safe behind the walls, but guilt followed fast behind. He could not bear to be comfortable while Antonio's fate remained unknown.

A cart slowly rumbled in front of him, pulled by a large,

shaggy, white goat, horns curling backwards from its proud head. A man, also shoeless, in a homespun suit, sat inside the bright red cart. Squid stared at him, and the man stared back at Squid from behind his mustache. The man tipped his hat at the priest, and continued on his way, whistling at the erstwhile goat to move on.

A few yards from the church, a man was busy digging, mounds of fresh earth surrounding him, crude, wooden crosses dotting the earth at his feet. Behind him was an obviously older cemetery with proper statuary and tombstones marking the dead.

An enormous shadow in the form of two dark wings enveloped the priest as he climbed up the steps. Fierce stone eyes stared down at Squid from above. The statue's muscles were frozen in movement as if ready to leap off its rocky perch. The angel's sword looked as though it was ready to come down on the boy. The snarling dragon beneath him was looking up, gaping its fangs in terror at the awaited blow.

"The same angel as the one on your medallion, Squid—Saint Michael. It was he who slew the dragon, another good omen," said Aldo, pointing at the boy's chest.

Squid bent his head back, staring deep into the angel's fiery gaze. "I don't need any more omens. What I need is to save my friend!" Squid shook his head. "I wish I knew what all this means."

"Cabral told me everything. I think this angel watches over

you. After all, it was a man from Saint Michael's very own island who rescued you."

"Antonio said the same thing," said Squid, stroking the medallion.

"Come inside," Aldo said.

Aldo strained to push open the heavy, green church doors, the scent of incense carrying past and overwhelming Squid's senses. He followed Aldo into the darkness, his eyes stinging slightly from the pungent smoke. The doors closed with a thud and they walked across the reflective marble floor.

"This is our holy church, founded by myself, when the village was still new."

Hundreds of burning candles lined the walls, making the interior glow an oily, rich gold. Another statue of Saint Michael stood at the front of the church, a wooden crucifix nailed to the wall behind it. Two ornately decorated pillars flanked the church altar, which curled up to the ceiling with a thousand different patterns carved in its polished oak.

A golden cross stood before the church's altar, a fist-sized ruby embedded in its decorative center. Light shone from the ceiling in golden shafts, enhancing the cross' sheen.

"We Portuguese are fond of our relics," mused the old priest. "Through art and the creative hand the path to God becomes illuminated."

Squid didn't answer the old man. He didn't feel like saying anything. A lump formed in his throat and his mind began to wander, grief and worry for his friend flooding over him.

"But I didn't bring you here for any sermon. I thought you would be interested in that." Father Aldo's bony finger pointed up towards the opposing wall.

The interior of the church was covered in a mosaic of white tiles, vivid blue depictions blazing out from them. The delicate swirls of an ocean were painted over a section, angels staring down from above.

A group of saintly men lay huddled along a ghostly blue shoreline, praying up to heaven. A group of ships were listing, broken in the distance. Longboats were lined up in the lattice of waves, the harpooners pointing with their spears at an emerging shape.

It looked almost like an island at first, a rock lifting out of a turquoise swirl. As Squid stepped closer he saw the reflective eye, blue and pearly in its center. Then he saw the tail, rippling along behind it. Little men were swimming away from its gape, pleading with the angels to save them. On the monster's back were dozens of lances, ropes tumbling out in tandem with the blue waves. Along the creature's side was the familiar gash, the flesh peeling back away from its hump.

"Lazarus!" Squid gasped.

"Oh yes. It's him," Aldo said from behind the boy. "Your ship was not its only victim. The old whalers painted this. Surprising isn't it, how talented these simple folk can be? I would take one of them over a hundred of those pampered fools from the city."

"Did you know Antonio's father? The whale took him too," Squid said.

"Yes. He was here in the beginning, long before the church, when this coast was little more than a collection of fishing cottages. The boy was never the same after his passing—Antonio, I mean. He had to grow very quickly, like many of the children of these islands. Too much death, too much sorrow … listen to me ramble on." Aldo sighed. "First I would like you to tell me about your ship, what you can make out from your damaged memory. Not the whaling vessel, understand me, but the first one. It was your family's ship, was it?"

"I don't remember. All I know is that Antonio found me, rescued me from Lazarus' jaws." Squid grimaced at the memory. Just saying Antonio's name made him pale.

Aldo rested a gentle hand on the boy's shoulder. "Are you sure? Could something else have happened?"

"What do you mean?"

"I mean there have been many stories about that whale, many exaggerations, let's say, but never has anyone claimed to see that particular whale ram a ship unprovoked."

"He attacked the pirate ship, that much I know for certain, and they're not whalers." Squid shrugged.

"Yes, I know. Perhaps the old thing has finally gone mad," said Aldo, staring at the tiled likeness of Lazarus. There was something youthful in the old man's gaze, despite the lines and creases, a playful quality in the way he looked at things. He was much like Antonio in a way. Despite this, Squid found Aldo's calm a bit maddening given the circumstances. Thoughts of Antonio brought back Squid's sense of urgency. He was desperate to get his friend back.

"What of Antonio? Are you going to leave him there? Will you do nothing for him?"

"I will wait a day for the pirates' anger to subside. Then I will implore the Dragon to release him," said Aldo.

"He won't," Squid said emphatically, increasingly irritated by the ancient priest. "Whatever he wants him for, he won't just give him up. You have to fight!"

Aldo frowned, leaning close with his long face. "I know you have lost much, my son. But do not despair, I beg you. Don't let their hatred and malice infect your heart. I wouldn't want that, and I doubt Antonio would either."

The old priest nodded knowingly, patting the boy's back.

"I have dealt with this Dragon before. He will soon leave these shores—I have prayed for this. Nothing can breach our walls, not even his cannons. No one is without a soul; no one is a complete monster. I will reason with him. It can be done," the priest consoled.

"Even if you can reason with him, there are other men on that ship, evil men. What if you're wrong?"

Aldo turned. Cabral and a couple of villagers appeared at the doorway, standing with their muskets waiting.

"Ah, the house!" Aldo exclaimed. "I had almost forgotten.

Antonio's family home lies empty—a simple cottage, but quite comfortable. I have arranged for you and your friend to stay there. Some of our people are busy airing it out as we speak."

Aldo made the sign of the cross over Squid's head, giving him a broad smile. With a wink he ushered the boy towards the big, green doors.

The light from the golden cross flashed before Squid's eyes, blinding him momentarily. He looked down at the church altar, Aldo kneeling before his relic, the turquoise whale peering at him from the wall with its pearly blue eye.

Squid descended the steps, past the shadow wings and jumbled wooden crosses.

Behind him the gravedigger was still digging, preparing the way for the dead.

SCRAB THE TERRIBLE

Responsibility can be a terrible thing. Scrab had been a pirate ship quartermaster for more years than he could count. No one ever doubted him. He was always successful in election and promotion. Promotion could only be had by vote—every pirate had a say in who he served under. Not surprising, given most pirates are deserters, escaping the lash and harsh rule of the Royal Navy or some such. You had to be respected, not just feared, to rise, and Scrab had risen far.

He pondered this fact, rubbing his tired, old knee. He twisted a knife in his hand, eyeing the big whaler's shadow, slumped in the darkness behind the whaler's cage.

Scrab could move quietly when he chose, but the careful movements took a toll on his joints.

"What are you staring at!" the whaler shouted.

Scrab shuffled down, his beady eyes shining through the blackness. "You've caused me a lot of trouble ..."

The whaler snarled, his big face pressed against the bars, daring the pirate to come closer.

His face was swollen, one eye slightly more shut than the other. Billy had kicked him on the head while they struggled. Dougan had been displeased upon learning of the harpooner's rough handling, and had punched poor Billy so hard he doubled over. It was a better fate than that of Scrab's old friend Lob and the fool Talbot.

Scrab shook his head as he remembered Lob, spread on deck, smoke rising from his black, gaping wound. Scrab shuddered at the image.

Lob had been reeling drunk before the captain, his one eye frantically searching the faces of his mates for help. The crew stood and watched Dougan calmly raise his pistol, cursing as he blew a hole in old Lob's chest.

Damn these islands, Scrab thought, staring into the whaler's grim face.

Scrab wanted the ship's cannons to thunder on the village, damn the women and children. Then off to sea to take their chances, hands filled with loot.

"Tell me of the church, whaler," Scrab hissed. "Is it gilded with the pretty gold, filled with treasure and old, saintly things?"

The whaler frowned. "Go to hell."

"One day, that's quite likely. But for now, tell me, is there gold? I hear of a cross, heavy with pretty gold and fit with a ripe, old ruby in the center."

"What do you know of it, you evil, old thing?"

"Secrets melt under my knife, whaler." Scrab smiled.

"Murderer," the whaler spat, the word rasping in his throat.

Scrab ran the knife over the bars. He nearly fell backwards when then whaler reached out for him.

"My, you're an angry sort! You'd sooner die with your secrets, eh, whaler? Fine then, suit yourself; sooner or later you'll feel the sting of my blade. Just you wait."

Scrab's eyes narrowed on the big man. "Why are you here, you think, whaler? Why is our dear Dragon keeping you alive, I wonder? Ransom maybe? You worth something back west? Lots of money in the whale oil business! No? Maybe someone with a purse is out there missing your particular set of skills?"

"Ha! Why would anyone pay for Antonio? I am a simple man, a harpooner. A God-fearing man, born and bred of these islands, and by God I swear I'll twist your old head off once I get out of here!"

Scrab chuckled. "Good luck to you, *Antonio*. Many have tried. I'll keep you in my prayers."

He turned before climbing the stairs, showing his

black-stained teeth. "Too bad about the boy, though. He'll die in that village, prayers or no! God won't be helping anyone in there."

Antonio roared, dust flaking off the rafters as he rattled the bars and shook the hold. "If you hurt that boy I'll tear this whole damn ship apart! I'll kill you, kill all of you!"

Scrab spat on the floor, turned and hobbled up the steps, cackling in the blackness.

He climbed up, his eyes straining, adjusting to the light. The men were sitting, a jug of Azorean wine being passed around. Between them lay a bowl of greasy goat stew. *Probably the last of the meat for a while*, thought Scrab.

"Bah! Stop drinking, you fools," Scrab hissed, kicking at them with his stump. "If this one gets out a second time, the captain will have your hides!" He knew, however, that it was a useless rebuke, as it was impossible to keep the men from drinking, especially in times such as these.

"Help," came a voice above him. Talbot was hanging by his feet from the mainmast. His bloated face was red and chafed by the sun. His lips were chalked white; his voice dry and cracked. He stared down with bulging eyes at Scrab. The old quartermaster barely recognized Talbot with his red beard cut away, flabby chins scraped and bleeding. Scrab found it strange to see him thus, a little funny even. Talbot was vain about his beard. It had amused the captain to have it cut away. Now Talbot looked pitiful and wretched, his flabby chin wobbling upside down.

"Sorry, mate," said Scrab, looking away.

"How long is he to stay up there?" asked a particularly scruffy looking shipman.

"Till he dies, I would imagine."

"Beggin' your pardon, Scrab, sir ... what's the captain thinking? Why in the blazes keep that big one below alive, while we string up our own sailing master?"

Scrab gave the shipman a grimace, squinting and pointing towards the upper deck. "Why don't you go up there and ask him yourself, lad?"

The shipman went pale, swallowed hard and stared at his boots.

"That's what I thought! He strung Talbot up because he failed him. He got himself knocked out and let those whalers escape. Don't be forgetting that."

"I'm not sure what's worse ... dying here, or drowning out there with that monster," the other pirate muttered.

Scrab sighed. "He's the very devil—we all know that! Captain's got a cruel streak running through his soul. He's got bloody hands, he does ... but damnation, haven't we all done terrible things, things past bearing? There won't be any heaven waiting for us, boys. Not here on these islands, out there or above, that's for sure."

Scrab licked his lips, scraping along the ground with his peg leg. Billy and some of the other men gathered up, agitated and curious.

"But we've never seen him licked," Scrab continued. "Never seen him lose a fight. He's gotten us out of more than a few tight spots, our pockets full of gold and loot! He'll see us through, lads … just you wait and see … ship's almost ready and that church up yonder is ripe for picking!"

"We've got little to show from these last raids, Scrab," complained a pudgy crewman, a pair of dangling earrings jangling from his lobes. "These islands haven't yielded much, and the ship's taken a real pounding. Our provisions are low to boot! We're sitting ducks, with no idea when another force from land or sea comes raised against us!"

"Help me," Talbot moaned, swinging with the creaking ropes, his fat body baking in the setting sun.

"Fine then, here are your choices, boys: you can mutiny, run for the wilds past those trees over yonder, or stand with your captain, the only man who can see us through this mess!" Scrab nodded as the men grew silent, happy with his little speech.

"*Please,* someone help me …," Talbot whimpered.

"Oh, for heavens sake!" Scrab yelled, pulling the knife from his belt and jumping up the mainmast. He heaved himself up with his arms to eye-level with Talbot.

"Please," Talbot whispered, his eyes moistening.

"Sorry," said Scrab, rather genuinely, as he dragged the knife under the fold of the fat man's chin.

Talbot gurgled and twitched, his shoulders trembling as

blood gushed out his throat onto the deck.

The men shuddered, stepping back from the blood flowing down on the deck like a waterfall.

Talbot's eyes rolled towards Scrab, and the old pirate spread his fingers over the sailing master's face. Hard as he was, Scrab didn't like watching the light go out of his victim's eyes. The jerking stopped and Talbot swung still and rigid.

Scrab snarled, closing the lids over Talbot's tortured gaze. He folded the tongue back neatly into the mouth, closing the jaw tight.

Scrab jumped down off the mast, hitting the deck with a thud.

"We do what we have to, lads. That's the way of it. No room for doubt and weakness." Scrab pointed his knife at the swinging body overhead. "Talbot's taught us that much!"

They gawked as he hobbled noisily to the captain's quarters. Big Billy cocked his head up at Talbot quizzically.

"Back to work with you!" Scrab roared, and the crew scattered.

The captain's quarters were rich with silks and fine things, glittering in the twilight breaking in streams through the grimy window.

Dougan sat, sinking lazily in his cushioned chair, a far-off look in his blue eyes.

A pipe lay overturned, smoking on the desk. Something

other than tobacco lay smoldering within it. Scrab was in luck! The Dragon was always easier to talk to after a few puffs of the strange smoke.

"What was all that about?"

"They're afraid!" Scrab hissed.

Dougan chuckled. "When are they not?"

"I'm more than a little put off myself! Did you have to kill Lob? Drunken fool, he was, but who on this ship isn't? And for what … those whalers?"

Dougan's face flushed. "I need them …"

"They're little more than peasants! These islands are full of them."

"I want these ones! That big one especially."

"Why?" said Scrab, pacing.

The captain followed him silently with his eyes.

"It's madness to stay here. We're in a bad way!" Scrab began earnestly. He was going to say more, but was stopped by Dougan, who raised a hand to quiet him.

"We won't be staying much longer, another tide or two at most."

Scrab froze. "What of the monster?"

Dougan smiled. "Don't worry your pretty head."

"And the village? How do we get past that wall? We need the provisions, and the gold from that church will go a long way with the men." Scrab's agitation did not seem to bother the captain at all, and the Dragon simply nodded and stroked his curly, cropped beard.

"Get some boats together and bring up the cannons. Careful and quiet-like, I want them on the beaches by morning."

Scrab gave a curt nod. "I sent Talbot on his way … he was making a fuss. I thought to make it quick, given circumstances."

Dougan waved at Scrab dismissively.

Scrab closed the door quietly behind him, sneezing suddenly from the captain's strange smoke. The western sky was beginning to glow crimson; men were busy scrubbing Talbot's blood from the deck.

Scrab leaned out the ship to stare for a moment. The island was a pretty thing, the beauty of it bringing up an unusual swell of emotion in the old quartermaster. The church blazed back at him, proud and gleaming in the fading twilight. A damp sweat crawled up his spine, familiar and comforting—the anticipation of blood and booty.

He rested a hand along the aft railing and listened to the lapping waves. Another sound rattled faintly in his ears, distant and barely there. He closed his eyes and cupped his ear; a slow, pulsing creak rippled in the water below. He looked out beyond the stern, seeing nothing.

The knot grew in his stomach, a feeling of foreboding slowly creeping through him.

"What kind of devil are you, whale? What has old Scrab ever done to you?" he groaned, softly to himself.

RESTING PLACE

The clicking echoed all around him; the salty water drained down his nose. He rose up to the light, his body floating amidst a swell. His arms ached heavily and he began to sink again, back into blackness. She reached out to him, the woman in white.

"Mother!" he tried calling, only to have more water sink into his lungs. His chest burned. He feared it would crack open, spilling his insides out.

The eye grew beneath him, a reflective orb pulsing in the darkness. The creature paused, closing its crooked jaw.

His mother floated past, lifeless before the monster. The beast swam after, nudging the body with its bulbous head. She didn't move, her legs and arms limp in the murky water. The creature clicked and creaked at the woman before it.

A new vision flooded his mind: he remembered hearing the sound of gulls and waves distinctly as the beast propelled him up, water rushing past him as the creature careened him forward. Then came the painful memory of his head spinning, blood oozing along the creature's back, his blood. He called out, still hoping she could hear him. "Mother!" Terror grew white in his mind, the panic blanking everything out. Then he remembered the black taking him, folding over him and shutting the world out.

Squid woke up screaming, Cabral shaking him.

"I'm sorry," he gasped.

"That was some dream!" Cabral grumbled. "Was it the ship? Jenkins?"

"No," Squid mumbled. "A memory, just a bad memory."

Cabral pulled away, hauling the musket over his shoulder. An axe, much like the one used in the longboats, dangled off his belt.

"I'm off to the wall."

"Can I come?"

"No! Stay, or rest. Play or something, like regular kids your age," Cabral barked, storming out.

Squid rubbed the sleep out of his eyes, sticking his tongue

out after Cabral.

The cottage was bare, made up of stones, green seeping through the cracks. A lizard crawled up the inside wall, flicking its tongue.

He reached under the straw bed, fumbling for his boot. He threw it with a thud against the wall, just missing the creeping lizard. It scampered away, nudging its slick body through a crevice. The tail wiggled nervously in the air before separating neatly from the lizard's body and falling to the ground.

Squid's face wrinkled as he got up to inspect the grisly, severed tail. He'd heard somewhere that lizards did this when cornered, the tail falling off at will when being attacked by a predator, but it was still an odd sight. Squid nudged the wriggling tail with his toe. The severed tail flicked wildly as he kicked it out past the crooked, old, wooden door.

Flecks of morning sunlight shone through the thatched ceiling, casting little rays into the damp darkness.

He pawed at his medallion, feeling for the angel's carved face and wings. It soothed him, having it close, feeling the rough edges of the metal. He closed his eyes, imagining his mother's face. But she was less than a ghost, the barest shadow of a memory, drifting in his mind.

A simple, wooden table sat in the corner with no chairs or stools around it. Pineapple, figs and dried sausage were spread out for him. A plate with a creamy, white cheese lay behind the spread.

A nest of birds chirped noisily in the straw overhead as Squid hungrily engulfed his meal. His taste buds erupted with flavor and pleasure, the sensation of enjoying a meal almost forgotten after hundreds of maggot-ridden servings on ship.

He stepped out to find one of the big dogs sitting on the doorstep.

"What are you doing here?" Squid exclaimed. The dog sat in front of him, cocking its massive head. "Alright, you can come along."

It barked, wagging its big rump. The dog stood, coming almost all the way up to his shoulders, salivating happily with long threads of drool.

The cottage sat above a hill, a little farther off from the rest of the village. The cliffs loomed tall overhead, birds spinning in lazy circles over the hanging trees. A dirt path led down the ridge, twisting and turning past the cemetery. Squid felt cut off here, ostracized from the rest of the village. He stood looking at the vast beauty of the sea and vegetation, wondering what it was like to grow up here, with both so little and so much all at the same time.

A cluster of tawny white feathers erupted from the cliffs, birds whirling acrobatically in the air over the cottage.

In the clear light he could see a squat building, farther up into the island's greenery. It was a windmill, stubby with a rocky foundation and slowly turning sails. It shone down blue and white over the landscape, a kind of marker atop the village of Luz.

Something swooped passed the squat structure. A large set of wings shot down towards him. Squid watched the hawk fly through the trees, over the dribbling, white waterfall.

It landed in the cemetery, a chubby bird crushed in its curling, black talons. Its probing eyes stared about, peering at Squid and the yawning dog at his side.

The hawk shook its bronze feathers and bent down, ripping at the little bird with its beak.

The dog whimpered as a small funeral procession slowly marched up the cobbled path. Four sturdy men carried a black coffin. Several women walked silently with them, chanting strange prayers and fumbling with heavy rosaries. Their black veils hung low over their faces, their voices shrill in what sounded like ominous warning. Their wooden shoes clopped clumsily down the trodden dirt path.

Behind the modest coffin, covered almost completely in white and blue flowers, an old woman was limping and sobbing, the beads of her silver rosary shaking in her fingers.

Father Aldo descended the church steps, children in white, lacy gowns holding the golden cross before him, spreading incense with every step.

The hawk fluttered and flew off, a ribbon of red flesh dangling off its claws as it soared.

The priest blessed the crowd, one of the children handing him a gilded bible. The sermon was in Latin, the words sounding grave and heavy to Squid's ears. The people seemed to understand, mouthing the words and responding when called for.

The dog nuzzled its big head into Squid's chest, the drool pouring out its drooping face in globs.

The old woman draped herself over the casket, her tortured cries ringing over Aldo's prayers as it was lowered into the yawning, black grave.

One by one the villagers filed past, solemnly dropping their flowers into the hole—hydrangeas, the same pinky-blue balls of bloom that seemed to grow everywhere on these Azores.

The procession filed away, the old woman still sobbing as she was carried off. Father Aldo returned to his church, the little children huddling behind him.

A lone figure remained, waiting over the grave. *Another old man. The island seems full of them,* Squid thought.

Squid made for the lower village, hoping to explore more of the place, maybe climb the wall and get another look at the pirate ship, if Cabral would let him. He was worried the ship might leave with Antonio on it.

The dog followed close behind Squid, walking briskly down the ridge. The old man stood waiting, staring at the boy, eyes opaque. Squid quickened his pace, hoping the old man would ignore him.

The old man wore his cap high over his wrinkled, ashen face. The skin seemed to hang over his big bones as he leaned against his cane. His hair was stark white, his big, crooked hands thick with blue veins.

"So, you, the boy!" he grinned.

"I'm a boy, yes. Nice to meet you," Squid said, quickening his pace.

"You've seen the whale then. The big one!" he shouted after.

Squid froze.

"I've seen him, too. Took my boat, he did."

Squid looked the old man up and down, his shoulders round and hulking, little scars crisscrossing his ancient hands.

"You were a whaler?" Squid replied.

"Yes, I was," he said in a thick, rough accent. "A good one too, like many here. And like many here, I have seen the whale, the scarred one … Lazarus. Yes. Yes, I have seen him."

The old man stared past the boy, his nose pointed up towards the sea, inhaling deeply. The big dog came up to him, sniffing at his hand for a scratch behind the ears. He chuckled, patting the dog on its muscled head.

"I miss it. Yes, I miss it."

"The sea?"

"The sea. The blood, yes, all of it. I miss it."

Squid bowed in deference to the old man, and turned to leave.

"I can still hear him!"

Squid turned.

"I can still hear him out there, every time I go out on the rocks. He waits for me, taunts me with his creaking throat. I alone survived on the longboat. He wants me out there. Wants to drag me down below with him, down, down into the black to finish what he started. I'm old now though, my bones will be buried in this earth."

The old man turned his head towards the boy, sniffing with his ancient nose.

"You've been close to him too … I can smell it on you, smell the stink of him … the salt and fishy rot of him!"

The old man's smile spread wider, showing off his soft, empty gums.

"He won't stop … he never stops, swimming and waiting in the black, ticking and clicking for you. He'll come. He'll come again for you, boy. You won't have to wait long."

The old man laughed and pointed up at the sea with his cane.

Squid shook his head, turning to leave, his palms damp as a chill ran up the back of his neck.

The dog trotted after him, through the jumble of houses and gardens in the village.

The shadow wings of the angel stretched long in the morning light, the stone angel following him with his eyes. The surroundings were still, the dog panting heavily in the hot morning air.

As Squid looked out at the shore from the high church steps, he could see the pirates were busy. They were crawling along like insects, their colorful sashes and headscarves contrasting brightly with the dark sand. Squid could see them dragging their heavy cannons along the beach.

The villagers were gathering at the bottom of the church, Father Aldo holding up his holy relic, the gold shimmering in the syrupy gold sky. The children stood below him as his staff stretched over the crowd and he yelled his Latin prayers.

Squid sprinted past the crowd, towards Cabral who was peering over the wall, leaning against his musket.

"What's happening?" Squid gasped.

Cabral pointed at a red figure striding along the shimmering beach with a long-sword.

"These Azoreans here have been digging a way out," said Cabral, eyes focused on the coast. "A tunnel leading out of the village and into the forest."

"I'm not leaving you," said Squid, flatly.

"You're going, get your mind right. This is no place for you," Cabral growled, still staring at the red figure.

The cannons boomed, men along the wall were screaming, smoke and ash billowing from the crumbling mortar.

"It's the Dragon," said Cabral, staring down at the climbing flames. "He's coming."

THE ANGEL AND THE DRAGON

Saint Michael the Archangel,
defend us in the day of battle.
Be our safeguard against the
wickedness and the snares of the devil.
May God rebuke him, we humbly pray,
and do thou, O Prince of the Heavenly Host,
cast into hell Satan and all the evil spirits
who prowl throughout the world
seeking the ruin of souls. Amen.

—THE CUSTOMARY PRAYER TO SAINT MICHAEL

The wall shook and rumbled with the cannons' booming; Squid could feel the mortar crumbling beneath his trembling fingers as each cannonball crashed into it.

Cabral gave him a shove and yelled, "Go!"

He turned to see the villagers screaming and gesturing towards the high cliffs. The pirates were climbing down like spiders, swinging from ropes and firing on the village below.

The tattooed giant, Billy, was leaping down the rocks, snarling and hooting with joy.

Stones disintegrated from the church's bright facade as a cannonball exploded against it.

The women and children fled towards the cemetery along the cobbled paths. The old man from the burial stood in the middle of them, staring at Squid from afar with his opaque eyes.

"Follow them and stay put! I'll find you!" Cabral shouted.

The red ship sailed with the dragon flag unfurled, the starboard gun ports opened up, yawning at the village.

More of the cannons were lined up on the grey beach, pounding the wall.

"Get down!" Cabral yelled, jumping on top of the boy.

The wall exploded, showering them with rocks and debris.

The booming was deafening. Squid's ears were ringing as the ground shook beneath him. He coughed up dust and rubbed soot from his eyes.

"You alright?" Cabral asked, loading his musket and fumbling with the powder.

Bodies were everywhere amongst the stones, gunfire cracking in the smoky air. Squid shook the ringing from his ears and felt for his medallion.

"I'm alright, I think. What about you, Cabral?" Squid shouted.

"I'm going to hold them off. Do as I say or by God, I'll whip you senseless!"

A hand grabbed at him, dragging him away. A stocky Azorean was pulling him along by the arm.

"No! Let me go!" Squid yelled.

Squid watched Cabral climb over the rubble, a pirate rushing straight for him as he crashed past the debris with his heavy axe. Cabral's musket flashed, and the pirate collapsed, with a red hole torn through him, at the African's feet.

A second pirate leapt over the body, straight into Cabral's bayonet. Cabral tore the musket away, cracking and breaking it over another's head.

He reached behind for his axe, swinging it wildly at the pirates, breaking through the breach. More Azoreans came up to help, driving the enemy back.

Screams echoed behind Squid, as fires spread though Luz's white homes and cottages. Thatch roofs erupted in pillars of flame, and villagers ran in panic.

Squid turned to see that a second battle was playing out beneath the cliffs, the Azoreans falling in heaps before Billy and his murderous crewmen. The pirates carried long pikes, jabbing and skewering them into the faces of anyone before them.

The old whaler from the graveyard was still waiting, standing still in the frantic swell of people. He held his ancient hand up and beckoned to the boy.

Squid felt his feet leave the ground as the man picked him up. A strange whizzing sound whirled past his ears. The Azorean collapsed and Squid fell hard to the ground beside him.

The Azorean's cap was blown off, red ooze began seeping from his open skull.

Squid picked himself up, seeing a cannonball thudding towards him. He ducked and the stone steps imploded behind him. The stone angel cracked, leaned slightly from his pedestal, but still stood tall.

Squid coughed up more of the black dust, smoke and ash misting his vision.

Cabral was a shadow atop the rubble. The red flag loomed over him, its dragon emblem blowing in the haze.

Squid could see the Dragon, now, taking long strides along the remaining wall with his sword. The blade flashed silver, but quickly become slick and red as the captain cleaved his way forward.

His pistol sparked and fizzled, the smoke obscuring his face and features. His uniform was damp with gore, red and fastened tight with brassy, gold buttons.

"Dragon! Dragon!" his men chanted, the bodies piling up beneath him.

Cabral climbed up to confront him, the axe swinging heavy

in his hands.

Dougan cut at the air gracefully, and Cabral fell back to avoid the sword. Cabral's axe came up just as quick, and the Dragon reared in surprise.

Squid doubled over with the force of a sudden blow. A twisted, ugly face, pockmarked and yellow, bore down on him.

"Come here!" snarled the pirate, swinging at him with his sword. Squid rolled, kicking the pirate in the chin.

The saber swooped over him, whizzing sharp in the air.

The man wailed as a dog, springing from the smoky steps, sunk its teeth into him.

Squid rolled back, kicking away the pirate's hand. The canine teeth sank into the pirate's neck and his legs writhed. The dog jerked its massive head, dragging the pirate into the ashen smoke from which it came.

Squid looked about in confusion. He clawed in the dirt, picked up the pirate's sword and ran. Grenadoes began popping all around him, belching fire and black powder.

Through the smoke, Squid saw plainly that Cabral was down, the Dragon looming, savoring the murderous blow.

Squid saw the sword fall, and the last of the wall crumbled in a heap of rocks. A cannonball broke through what remained of the defense, crashing over the bodies of the defenders. The pirates were sent flying; the captain jumped and rolled adeptly from the explosion.

The dust settled and Squid could see no sign of his friend.

Cabral was buried, entombed beneath a wreckage of black stones.

The captain rose, shaking the mortar off his crimson uniform. The men raised a cheer and howled his name, "Dragon! Dragon!"

Panic and rage boiled inside Squid, flooding his thoughts. Gritting his teeth, he wiped the stinging tears from his eyes. Only a few remaining shadows remained, fleeing before the red Dragon's victory. The dog was gone, the body of its victim lying in a ghastly heap on the cobbles.

From behind the black wings of Saint Michael he saw a glimpse of the church's light. He hadn't seen Father Aldo. Squid hoped he was still alive, still praying in his church.

Squid bolted up the steps and past the big, tilting statue. He flung the doors open and found Aldo alone, kneeling on the bare marble, staring up at his golden cross.

"Father!" Squid yelled. "You have to go! The village is burning! They're everywhere!"

The old priest wouldn't turn.

"And where am I to go?" he said calmly. "This is my home, my church."

Squid ran up and shook him. "No! You have to run! You have to try!"

Father Aldo grabbed him roughly by the shoulders. Then he smiled and placed his old hand on the boy's chest. "It's you who must run. Run and live, be happy in these islands, my boy.

Father Aldo stays here, his old bones to rest eternally in this holy house. My island, my village, my home."

Squid stepped back, shaking in horror.

Father Aldo stared back at him, his youthful eyes seeming suddenly very old and tired. He nodded solemnly, blessing the boy with a quiet, little gesture.

Squid retreated backwards towards the door, his chest heaving with indecision.

The church doors shook with a violent knocking. Father Aldo stood, pointing towards the altar.

"Hide!" he hissed, suddenly anxious.

The cross above them glittered as Squid shrunk behind the table's lacy cloth. Heavy footsteps thumped across the marble floor.

"There is nothing for you here, my son. This is a house of God!" he heard Aldo say.

Squid squinted through the tiny lattice holes of the cloth, the Dragon blazing red over Aldo's black form.

The sword rose again. Aldo continued to kneel with his hands clasped in final prayer. The blade made a zipping sound as it cut through the robes. The old priest crumpled on the marble floor, his blood tracing the lines of its stone veins.

Squid held his hand to his mouth, tears flooding his eyes.

"Hello!" came a voice behind him, throwing the table back.

It was Scrab, grinning madly with the golden cross in his grip.

"No, you can't have it!" Squid yelled, pointing his sword.

Scrab simply slammed the base of the cross against Squid's head with a quick, violent blow.

The sword fell with a clank and Squid reeled. The old wound cut open, singing with pain across his brow. He felt the cold marble beneath him, the smells of incense mixing with iron and gunpowder.

His head was drumming, a white light expanding in his mind, a flood of memories and sensations. A face appeared in his thoughts, a kind and gentle face: it was his mother, calling for him in the darkness. Her black hair swirled in the water and she beckoned, "Come, Daniel, come. It's time to go home."

He began floating, flying over the islands; they shrunk like emerald pools in the ocean below. The clouds were moulding into shapes, swelling with colors and sounds. The image of a port spread before him, the boats bobbing along the docks. The sounds of gulls and teeming crowds resounded in his ears. He remembered now … a home nestled along the English coast, a father long dead and forgotten. He felt for his mother's hand as they boarded the merchant ship. Her demeanor was dignified, but her clothes were worn and tattered. She smiled, hiding the desperation in her eyes. There was no life on that crowded coast. No livelihood, no future, just a mad press of people, clawing and climbing over each other. They were leaving all that for the Americas—a new world, fresh with new life and hope.

Then came the fire, the clouds clumping into great wafts of

black smoke and flame. The ship was broken, cracking beneath them, men laughing across the water, staring gleefully from their red vessel. His mother pleaded, but still they laughed. A flag waved in the wind, the black dragon in a field of red. A man stood beneath it, tall and red, looking calmly out at their sinking wreck. A black figure stood beside him, dark and hunched, like a gargoyle.

Squid remembered diving into the water, the ship crashing in flames overhead. There was blood and pain, his mother disappearing into the blackness beneath him. He wanted to go down deeper, to follow her, but found that he couldn't, the urge to breathe too strong. The great eye hovered below, watching patiently. He remembered the first great intake of air, the relief as the whale bore him up. The whale rumbled and creaked as it carried him away. It spat great jets of foam into the sky. And then they met another ship, its white sails billowing towards them.

The clouds separated. Squid's visions grew distant, and Antonio's voice whispered to him from the haze. Another memory, fresh and strong in his mind … "Easy now. Antonio will take care of you. You're safe now, boy …"

Squid's eyes fluttered, consciousness piercing through him. The dream was gone. Scrab was staring down at him.

"Get up, boy! You don't want to miss all the fun, do you?" said Scrab. "Your friend that Portuguese whaler, what was his name … Antonio? He misses you something awful."

Scrab had the cross in the crook of his arm, and was cackling as he dragged the boy limply down the steps. Rough hands pulled him up as more of the pirates circled around the boy, with sticky, red faces.

The Dragon was there, slinking under the shadow wings, red and terrible to behold.

Everything seemed black now, the village empty and smoldering. Only the angel remained, staring back mutely at him from its tilting angle. Squid kept his focus on Saint Michael as he was led away. Fire licked at the base of the statue, the angry face wreathed in flame.

NO ESCAPE

"Leave him up there, Mr. Scrab. I want the crew to get a good look," Dougan growled, freshly bathed clean of his gore.

Talbot's body was bloated, black and reeking atop the ship, flies buzzing furiously as the gulls feasted on his rot.

Scrab shuffled away sheepishly, cradling his new relic like some lucky talisman.

"Such should be the fate of all weak men," Dougan grumbled, admiring the body.

The captain stood at the stern, cursing the retreating islands under his breath. He intended to sail until they were far from view.

"Well, Mr. Scrab? Any sight of the monster?" Dougan barked.

"No, Captain, clear sailing this time it seems."

The skies were crisp blue and the islands were slowly slinking away, foggy, grey shapes in the distance. The waters were calm, calmer than the crew had seen in weeks. There wasn't a whale in sight. Once they cleared the Azores, they would surely be free of the monster whale.

Dougan sneered at Scrab, who was stroking his precious cross, happy with his new prize.

"You're a superstitious fool, Scrab. What can that trinket possibly do for us? Melt it down soon as you are able!"

"It's a thing unnatural—holy, Captain. So the islanders say. Perhaps it will keep the beast at bay."

Dougan huffed, "Damn your eyes. You're an idiot, Scrab."

Scrab peered back cautiously from under his hat. "That body's been up long enough, hasn't it, Captain?"

"A reminder, Mr. Scrab. The crew's grown soft, fearful as old women. I'm no phantom or sea monster. They'd do better saving their fears for me."

"Aye," Scrab gulped, fumbling backwards with the ship's sudden shudder, struggling to regain his balance.

A man fell from the foremast, splashing into the water just off the bow.

"Fire the cannons!" Dougan shouted.

The creaking rippled through the swell. The wrinkled, grey shape of Lazarus, the monster whale, breached ahead of the ship. The man in the water waved his arms as the ship sailed past with the wind. The whale's crooked jaw cut along the water behind him as he screamed his last breath.

"Kill it! Damn you!" yelled Dougan, the whale diving away from the cannons' roar, its tail rising as it sank beneath the booming ship.

"What damage, Mr. Scrab?" Dougan gritted.

"None that I can tell as of yet, Captain. He's jerking us around a bit is all. That's the extent of it, I think!" Scrab screeched, holding his cross all the tighter.

Dougan slapped him across his head, sending his hat tumbling down the deck. "Fool! Get me that whaler!"

The whale erupted out of the ocean, the swell rocking the pirate ship from side to side. It lay on the surface, at least a mile out, slapping at the water angrily with its mighty tail. The crew stared back in fear and wonder.

Lazarus was waiting for them: smacking the water furiously, goading the pirates on.

Antonio was brought up. The whaler stood larger than most of the pirates, aside from Billy, that is, who was eyeing the man cautiously.

Dougan admired Tony. He saw before him a whaler whose hands were strong like granite, and whose face looked like it had been carved from rock. Antonio walked straight and tall, his hulking shoulders pulled back. It had taken five of the crew to subdue and drag him out of the hold, even with Billy holding a pistol to the man's head.

A smile spread across Dougan's attractive face. This whaler was just the sort he needed.

"Here he is then, Captain," bowed Scrab. "A worthy sacrifice, no doubt."

Dougan pointed towards the whale. "What can you tell me about that thing?"

"It's a whale," Antonio grumbled.

Scrab slammed his pistol against the back of Antonio's head.

"Very big whale," Antonio said, wincing only slightly, ignoring the blow.

"What do you know about it? And if this next answer doesn't please me I'll skin you alive."

Antonio shrugged.

"I'll peel my answers from you, if I have to," the Dragon spat.

"Go ahead. Best be quick, too. We'll all be going down soon enough. Straight to the bottom." Antonio chuckled.

The pirates paled.

Dougan motioned up to the mainmast. "Are you sure you won't reconsider?"

Antonio stared at Talbot. "Go ahead, and kill me then. What's one more dead body? My village and my friends are all gone and you expect favors of me? You can all sink. I'll have my hands around your neck as we go under, God willing."

Dougan threw back his head in wild laughter, "By thunder, you're fun! What I could do with ten such as you."

Antonio horked and spat, the thick wad landing on Dougan's boot.

Dougan inched closer to the whaler's face, Billy's shadow creeping up behind him.

"Bring me the boy!"

A trickle of dried blood was caked along the side of Squid's head. He was shaking, despite the heat, a blue pallor tinting his trembling lips.

"Squid!" Antonio yelled. Three crewmen had him by the arms, Billy's pistol cocked and loaded.

Scrab was grinning behind the boy and pointing a knife to his throat. Squid mouthed the words, "I'm sorry." His grey eyes were dull, expressionless.

"Let him go! He's just a boy! What kind of men are you?" Antonio seethed.

"We're just simple pirates here, whaler, just trying to get by," Scrab croaked.

"Shut up, Mr. Scrab!" yelled Dougan, quickly diverting his attention back to the whaler. "Easy now, no need to get upset. Now, tell me about that whale … please."

Antonio scowled at Scrab, who twisted the knife in his splotched hand.

"What do you want to know?" Antonio sighed.

"What do you know about it? Tell me, or you'll see your

little friend's brains strewn over my deck," said Dougan in a cool drawl.

Antonio frowned, closing his eyes. "The old whalers have spoken of it for years. Lazarus, they call him, because no matter how often you lance him, he returns … rising fresh from the dead, it seems. I can't remember a time when I wasn't hearing tales of him. Every so often a death would be blamed on the monster. There was one man from my youth, a big fellow by the island's standards. He had lost both legs, not from the rope or accident, but from the teeth of that monster. I myself never gave my father's stories much credit. I thought it an animal like any other. I've seen many whales and they never cease to impress—immense and wondrous, strange beasts, they are. He's a bull you see, and all bull sperm whales are dangerous, often turning to attack the boats, even a ship on occasion. The chances of your longboat staying afloat are only half best when you go out to lance a whale."

Antonio paused and licked his lips.

"The old whalers say Lazarus is immortal, a demon, God's punishment for all the killing man has done against these passive whales of the sea. Many whaling ships disappeared around our islands in my father's time. The old men always blamed Lazarus. Always that whale, even earthquakes were blamed on the thing. Strangely, the regular ships had stories of their own. Lazarus would swim by, rolling past them all gentle. It never attacked a merchant or fishing vessel, saving its anger for the whalers alone. God's judgment, they affirmed, a beast brought up to deliver the sea's justice."

Antonio paused, his face taking on a faraway look. "It took my father, then my own ship."

The pirates crowded around him, captivated by the whaler's story.

"Enough about your daddy! What about the cross? Can the cross save us, perhaps?" asked Scrab, quickly holding it up.

"No chance of that. What would you be able to do with it, damned as you are!" Antonio scowled.

Scrab seemed to shrivel, the knife trembling in his fingers.

"What is your professional opinion then, Whalemaster? Is this animal a thing of heaven, hell or earth?" asked Dougan.

"Oh, I think it's a whale alright, an old and freakish one, no doubt. You see, a whale is a thinking animal. It's as smart as any man. I've seen whales do things that would make your hair stand on end. I've seen the whale killers chase a right whale for days, just for a nibble of the big thing's face. Others make a net of bubbles to confuse and disorient fish, clustering them in huge swarms before swallowing them whole. There's endless strange varieties of whales, you know. One has a horn protruding out its head, a tooth, grown long for jabbing with. This whale uses its tooth like a tool to break through ice, a strange kind of unicorn, some call it. The ivory is worth a pretty penny, but I've never been so lucky. There's tell of whales up north so old they've outlived three generations of men. Perhaps this freak has a touch of the same longevity."

Antonio held up his hands and turned towards the gawking crew. "Have you ever seen a sperm whale's brain? No animal in all of nature compares; it's the largest. This one, I think's been driven mad, either by age or pain. You've seen the wound on its side? It won't heal; it festers, driving the whale's rage and purpose."

Antonio pointed at the whale. "You see what it's doing? Slapping the water with its tail. It speaks to you, dares you. They have many ways of talking with one another, just as we do. Sometimes it smacks the water just like so, a kind of warning, I think. This beast is out here alone. I should know; my ship was sailing these waters for months. I think the whale herded the others away. It threatens, but it doesn't want to attack unless it has to. It hopes you'll go back, but will most likely strike before long."

"We can't go away. We've overstayed our welcome on those islands. What if we ignore it and keep sailing? You said it wouldn't attack anything but a whaling ship. So why stalk us?" said Scrab.

Antonio pursed his lips. "You're very much like a whaling ship, big enough, too. You even smell and act like one."

"How so?" asked Dougan.

Antonio gestured to the body swinging overhead, the gulls squawking in mad circles for a taste of it. "Death. Your ship reeks of it. And blood, there is always lots of blood on a whaling ship."

"Will it attack and aim to drown us?" asked Scrab anxiously.

"Yes. It sank my ship and it was filled with better men than I see here."

Scrab grunted and pressed the knife a little closer to Squid's Adam's apple. Antonio clenched his jaw and raised his hand apologetically.

"So tell me then. How do we kill it?" Dougan growled.

Antonio smiled. "Pick a few dozen men from your crew, the strongest. Get them to sail out on the boats with as many spears and sharp things as they can carry. When they're close to the beast get them to throw everything they have at it. If they're lucky, only most will die. When the beast tires, jab at it quickly, try to hit its lungs or heart. Then wait and pray. Singing can help you drive out the fear, works for me. Try to sing if you can."

Dougan cocked his head to one side, his lids hanging heavy over his icy eyes. "Kill it for us, and we'll free you and the boy."

Scrab opened his mouth in shock. Dougan gave him a scowl and the old pirate clamped his face shut.

"Don't listen to them!" Squid shouted, knocking the knife away.

Antonio squared his huge shoulders. "Give me back my harpoon. We'll see what I can do."

THE EYE

"You won't need those, not out there. You'll have to leave them," Antonio said, sharpening his harpoon. "No sense in weighing down the boats further."

"To hell I will," grimaced the rakish looking pirate, holding up his sword and pistol.

"You'll do as he bloody well says!" thundered Captain Dougan. "He'll be your master on that boat, do you hear? Do as he commands and kill that whale!"

The men shuffled forward, piling their swords at Dougan's feet indignantly.

"Show that blasted whaler what you're made of, lads!" Scrab encouraged.

They boarded the boats, five in all, and waited for the Whalemaster. Squid had noticed that Antonio had picked the biggest men to row at the bow, his makeshift harpooners. Billy was first, trembling with his hand at the oar. Several other men had their heads tilted over the side of the boat, vomiting into the sea as fear overtook them.

Squid watched as Antonio inspected Cabral's longboat, still hoisted up the side. He reached over and ran his hand over the hull. "These other dinghies won't be as fast, slow even," he told Dougan. "But fear not, that whale's not going anywhere. I'll head straight for him on this longboat … when the time's right. The others will hang ready."

The cannons gave a mighty crack, firing iron balls and jets of water into the air. The whale dove and rolled in lazy circles, still waiting for the boats to head out.

"I wish to speak with the boy," Antonio said.

Dougan nodded and Scrab inched away from Squid.

"My name is Daniel," Squid blurted, Antonio kneeling down next to him.

"So you remember now! That's good," Antonio said, stroking the boy's hair.

"They're all gone, Tony—my mother and Jenkins. I saw Cabral fall before the wall, buried beneath the stones. They're all dead. We're alone now."

Antonio hugged Squid, big drops of tears rolling down his stony face.

Squid shook his head. "I think the village is gone, Tony. I saw it burn. I don't know if anyone survived. I just don't know." He gulped.

"You're alive, that's good. That's the important thing. You must be brave for a little longer, Squid … Daniel," Antonio croaked through the lump in his throat.

"Enough of this!" Scrab bellowed.

"A moment!" Antonio growled, thumping the end of his harpoon against the deck.

"The whale, Tony! Don't kill it!" Squid whispered. "It isn't evil. He saved me, Antonio. These men sunk my ship and watched my mother drown. They killed her! They're the real monsters … the Dragon, Scrab and the rest. I would have died too, if not for Lazarus carrying me up on his back … You said it happened sometimes, the dolphins, remember? You have to believe me."

"What are you saying?" Antonio gasped.

Squid nodded, "It's true, Tony! I remember, all of it."

Antonio stroked the long scar that ran down Squid's forehead, flaking off the last dried clumps of blood.

"It doesn't matter now. We have no choice."

"Wait!" Squid yelled. "Take this."

The boy reached into his shirt and pulled out the medallion.

"Who searched the boy?" Scrab yelped, snatching the

medallion out of Squid's hands. "Oh, a pretty thing!" he smiled with greedy eyes.

Dougan walked up and yanked it from him. "We don't have time for this. Let the whaler take it. He'll need it."

The captain handed the medallion to Antonio and patted Scrab consolingly on the head.

"Kill that whale, and you're free," Dougan cooed, a reptilian smile creeping over him.

Antonio held up his harpoon and grunted, then calmly loaded the longboat with his two remaining harpoons. Three gangly crewmen followed in after him, pale and shivering.

The boats bobbed along the water, the pirates keeping close to the ship, their faces dripping with a slick, cold sweat.

The whale hung still before them, its tail lying motionless beneath the water, its bulk nodding against the waves.

Squid peered down at Antonio and nodded. Antonio stroked the medallion on his chest, pointing with his harpoon.

"Row! Bring me to him, you dogs!" he barked out at the pirates, their trembling hands white against the oars.

He had instructed the men to separate a half-mile apart, and meet the whale in the classic arch formation. The pirates hesitated, staring up at their captain. None of them had signed on for this. Dougan whistled, waving them forward like a master would do his dogs.

"I'm your captain now! Do as I say if you want to live!" Antonio railed. "Row! Row for your lives! Row for your cursed ship and your damned souls! Row or die, into its teeth! Row, damn you! Row!"

Billy steadied himself nervously at the front of his dinghy. The pirates followed Antonio's boat, plowing through the waves towards the awaiting monster.

The water was shimmering blue and calm, only the sounds of oars and swooping gulls disturbing the eerie peace.

Squid watched nervously as they came within a few meters of Lazarus, and Antonio held up his hand for the boats to stop. The whale let out a long, rippling creak. The boats stood waiting and the whale sat watching—a jet of water sputtering angrily out of its blowhole.

"Stand up!" Antonio roared.

With shaking legs, each of the four unlikely harpooners stood gripping their long pikes. Billy's boat rocked wildly under him. He was too heavy for such a tiny thing. He held two pikes in each hand, screaming madly at the top of his lungs.

There would be no rope in this battle with the whale, only the naked iron.

The whale sank, leaving a gentle ripple on the ocean's surface.

Antonio turned and gestured at his oarsmen, who began rowing backwards, behind the line of dinghies.

Billy seemed to peer down at the monster's shadow, the other men staring back at Antonio in confusion.

The whale breached like thunder beneath the line of dinghies. It rose and splintered three of the vessels with its big head.

Men flew into the air.

"What's he doing?" Scrab yelled from the deck of his ship, squeezing the back of Squid's neck. "You'd better hope he dies out there, boy, or by thunder I'll have him strangled before your eyes!" Scrab hissed.

Antonio's longboat slowed a few yards from the jumbled wreckage, strewn like matchsticks in the water. He crouched at the bow, his harpoon hoisted on his shoulder, looking tense and ready.

The whale thrashed its tail at the remaining dinghies, throwing the pirates headlong into the water. Billy sank his pikes firmly into the whale's head, blood spewing out from the monster's mouth.

The beast rolled past, towards a dozen or so of the floundering crewmen who were swimming desperately for safety. The whale's pale teeth glimmered in the blue, its jaw skimming the surface and sucking the men up. Tortured screams reached high over the ship, as the pirates were ground down the whale's throat.

Squid watched as Billy moved around wildly in his boat, searching for anything to throw. He seemed to be looking desperately at Antonio, but the whaler was hanging back just far enough away from Lazarus' last strike. Billy gave a panicked shriek.

Antonio remained silent and still.

"He's using them as bait! Damn him!" Scrab cursed.

The jaw came around, the whale's rotten breath fouling the

air. The crooked mouth snapped at Billy's boat, and the crew flung themselves over as the planks snapped beneath them.

"Now!" Antonio shouted to his pirate crew, coming up along the whale's side. His harpoon flew heavily over Billy, the tattooed man's body broken between the whale's teeth.

The beast's shadow sank in a pool of inky red. A severed arm, covered in black markings, floated up for a moment, then slowly began following the whale down below.

"Oh, Billy," Scrab moaned.

"Quiet, Mr. Scrab," Dougan snapped, his gaze fixed on the remaining longboat.

Antonio shouted in Portuguese at the waves, as if daring the monster to rise back up.

Lazarus burst out, crashing back and forth, flailing with pain. Blood was spurting out of its blowhole, cascading like a fountain down its bulbous head.

It made a rattling sound, the crooked jaw hanging open. It crashed sidelong against the water and thrashed madly with its tail.

Antonio stood watching, one leg propped up against the bow of his longboat.

His harpoon was lodged in the beast's eye, bobbing at an odd angle.

Squid covered his ears at the agonized clicking, tears running down his face.

"You're a strange one," muttered Scrab, a look of disgust on his face. "Why should you care for a monster like that? Be grateful your friend *might* come out of this alive."

Squid wiped his tears, looked again at the whale, now swimming in blind circles, the waters foaming pink all around it. Lazarus rolled, showing the long, white gash that ran along its side and the many scars that covered its wrinkled blubber.

Lazarus turned, staring back at the red ship with its remaining eye.

"Row!" Antonio bellowed, his tiny crew shaking their heads. "Row, damn you! Bring me to him before he recovers!"

The men rowed nervously onwards, the whale's rasping breaths rattling in the air.

Antonio aimed, the boat skimming alongside the whale's oily, long body. The tail came up and Lazarus dove just as Antonio let fly the long shaft, which darted in the water after him.

The waters rippled over the beast's enormous shadow, the air still and electric over the ship. Its body floated back up, massive and grey. The jaw hung crooked and still. Antonio and his men rowed over and tore the harpoon from the whale's dead eye.

He examined the wound. Nodding, he held up the red harpoon for all to see.

Antonio pulled back, as if for a final jab, but hung back as the whale quickly sank before him. The old ropes swirled after the creature, vanishing into the bloody, black sea.

The pirates cheered, giddy with laughter as they hugged one another. They hooted, flinging their caps in the air.

Squid looked out at Antonio and his bloody harpoon, burying his face in his hands.

"Ha! No need to cry little one. You'll all be together soon." Scrab smiled.

Antonio boarded the ship, the pirates at his longboat's oars shaking with relief. His shoulders slumped, a look of defeat and resignation on his chiseled face. The straggle-toothed pirates at his side were beaming, grateful to be alive.

Dougan walked over to him, looking him up and down. "I said nothing about using my men as bait. Your boat and crew are all that survived."

Antonio held the captain's gaze. "You wanted the whale dead, no? I warned you there would be few left alive, even if we were lucky."

The captain chuckled and waved his hand dismissively. "No matter, the bargain was struck and you kept your end."

"What about Billy?" Scrab interjected.

Antonio frowned at the old pirate. "Honor the agreement!"

The pirate crew crowded, glaring menacingly. Antonio still had the harpoon, held at his side.

"Now, now, my boys," hushed Captain Dougan. "We're sportsman-like men, are we not?"

Dougan's smile evaporated, his face freezing into a cold grimace. "Mr. Scrab!" he yelled. "Bring the boy to his master. It's time they were freed."

Scrab dragged Squid forward, keeping a firm grip on his arm. The old pirate reached out for the medallion, but Antonio quickly slapped the hand away.

"Oh, come now. No hard feelings," said Captain Dougan.

Squid leaned over and whispered to Antonio, "They mean to kill us now, Tony."

Scrab licked his lips. "Smart lad."

The crew laughed.

"Oh no, we wouldn't dream of it," said Dougan. "We're going to free you into the sea, what happens then is entirely between you and your maker ... or the sharks."

"You killed my mother!" Squid blurted, struggling free of Scrab. "You killed her and sank our ship!"

The men hung back for a moment, confused. A look of wonder passed over Dougan, his eyes taking on a curious, eager expression.

Antonio pointed his harpoon at the captain, his eyes shifting over the many faces of the crew.

"The ship was on fire! You could have helped her! You could have saved us! But you did nothing! You laughed and watched us drown! You're the real monsters, not that poor creature out there. It was always you!" Squid shouted, the words tumbling out of him.

Dougan frowned, cocking his head from side to side as he examined the boy. His hand traced the outline of the scar on

Squid's head in a slow, reverent movement. Then his head flew back in full laughter.

The Dragon's laughter bellowed in Squid's ears, fueling his anger. Without thinking, Squid reached into his pocket, the sharp and smooth scrimshaw tooth from Jenkins was still there.

Scrab howled as Squid jabbed the tooth into his thigh, tripping backwards on his peg leg.

Antonio swung his harpoon, cutting down three of the circling pirates. A pistol fired, one of the crew getting a shot off before crumpling beneath his iron. His aim went wide, the ball tearing into Scrab's cheek.

The crew moved in and dozens of axes, pikes and pistols bore down on Antonio.

Scrab howled in pain; the shot had torn his cheeks to pieces, passing straight through one side of his mouth and exploding out the other. He staggered up, cradling his golden cross for comfort.

The metal of the Dragon's sword seemed to sing as he drew it from the scabbard. He held it straight—it shone with a silver glint in the bright sun.

His eyes sparkled blue, deep and fathomless as the sea, pitiless and cold. "Kill them!" he hissed.

Antonio shielded Squid behind him, his knuckles white—harpoon ready.

Suddenly, the ship jostled, the waters frothing all around them.

Squid was saved from falling by Antonio, who had braced himself against the railing and steadied him. The crew tumbled everywhere, rolling along the swaying deck.

Squid stared out. A massive head was pulling away from the *Red Gull*. The ship began listing to starboard, a large hole in its side with water rushing in.

Lazarus was rising, his fury terrible and great.

THE BEAST RISES

The sound of the whale's clicking grew, rising like an electric pulse over the ship.

Men slid off the deck and crashed into the ocean below. The whale's mouth was waiting, gaping and ready to take them in.

Squid held on tight to Antonio, whose harpoon was spiked into the timbers, keeping them from toppling forward onto the careening deck.

Scrab cradled the mizzenmast, screaming at his mates for help.

Flames crackled from the aft of the ship. The captain's quarters had caught fire, his silks and finery glowing from within.

A pillar of billowing smoke rose from the ship and swirled into the sky. The whale's eerie call mingled with the splintering cracks of the breaking ship.

"Man the cannons!" yelled Dougan, climbing what was left of the quarterdeck and bellowing futilely at his crew. There was no one to heed his orders, many had fallen overboard and the rest were holding on for dear life to the doomed ship.

The ship rocked and lurched, the mainmast crashing over everyone still on deck, breaking crossways over the ship. The riggings lay strewn along the deck, men gasping beneath the tangles of ropes.

The whale pushed against the splintered hull with its head, cannons and crew spilling out into the sea.

The captain was thrown back over the railing, still gripping his long-sword as he held on.

"Back, you devil!" shouted Scrab, holding up the golden cross.

He had propped himself up on his wooden leg and was pointing the holy thing at the monster. Scrab's face was a mess of red, torn flesh, teeth and gums peeking through the gaping streak along his cheek.

"Back to hell with you!" he yelled.

A pistol skidded under Squid's feet. He stooped to pick it up. The hammer was cocked and loaded, the powder still miraculously dry. His hand was still as he aimed it at Scrab's face. The pirate stared back with hollow, black eyes.

"No!" Antonio shouted, lifting the pistol as it sparked and fired. "Leave him, boy! Leave the evil man be … he isn't worth it, boy."

Squid nodded, choking back his tears.

The ship vibrated and the bowsprit split from the ship, the wood groaning like a wounded beast.

Scrab stood, spitting blood and blackness, a tall shadow looming over him. The mountain of grey, tattered flesh had risen up out of the sea. The whale's tail fanned, blotting out the sun.

Scrab held up the cross with trembling fingers. "Be gone, demon! Go back down below, where you came from. Back to hell, I say!"

Scrab shook the useless trinket as the tail rose, crashing over him, and slamming him flat against the deck.

The tail slid back into the water, leaving a trail of gore as it went. Scrab's hat fluttered past the shattered deck, the golden cross skidded along its slippery surface.

"Scrab!" yelled Dougan, dragging himself up.

A horrible snapping sound echoed from below as the ship began breaking apart, flames billowing high on the upper deck.

The captain shook his fist at the whale. "Damn you! Damn you, monster!"

The broken ship was splintering into the sea. Squid noticed the captain eyeing him and Antonio, who were propped up on the raised timbers, fumbling with the ropes of the longboat.

"You! You caused all of this! You cursed my ship, bringing this monster with you!" Dougan spat.

"It's over! Leave him alone!" Antonio yelled, water lapping at his boots.

"I'll kill the both of you! By God, I'll have my last kill!" Dougan bellowed, his eyes red with the fire's glow. He moved towards them, crawling up the shattered deck, his face contorted with murderous hate.

Squid struggled with the knots, the ship listing, now almost completely to starboard. The *Red Gull* was cracking in two separate pieces, as the whale continued to shove hard against the hull.

Dougan leapt towards them with his sword, snarling like an animal. Antonio swung wide, nearly losing his balance.

The whaler skidded, Squid tumbling after him, grasping at the tangled riggings.

"Take my hand!" Squid yelled at Antonio. The whaler was holding tight to the shattered mizzenmast with his free hand, the floorboards splintering beneath his embedded harpoon.

"Behind you!" Antonio shouted.

Squid turned, the fire's heat licking at his back.

The Dragon was clawing his way up towards him. "I'll have you now. I'll have your blood before we go under!"

Antonio grabbed the ropes and dragged himself up, climbing over to Squid.

The Dragon slashed. The sword sparked, breaking against

the harpoon's iron.

Antonio kicked from above the ropes, clipping the captain hard under the chin with his boot.

Dougan pulled a pistol. It belched fire and smoke. Antonio veered, the ball ripping through his jacket.

Antonio recovered his balance quickly, swinging his heavy weapon.

Antonio's harpoon cut into the captain with a sickening crunch, pinning him to the sidelong deck. The once handsome features of the captain were distorted, now bulging under the whaler's squeeze as Antonio pressed on his windpipe.

"I'm going to kill you," Antonio growled, bringing his face up close to Dougan's.

The captain's blue eyes glazed with fear, his long, elegant hands clawing uselessly at the harpooner's iron grip.

Antonio wrenched the harpoon from Dougan's body, pulling him up by the neck.

Squid looked up at the rage in Antonio's face, the scar glowing white under his chin, nose flaring wide. It wasn't the face of the man he knew, the father he wanted.

"Tony! You were right … don't. We're not like them," Squid said, his face pleading and tender.

Antonio growled, "That boy is worth ten of you."

Dougan hissed, a long, rattling breath and his eyes rolled white. Antonio picked him up by his uniform and flung him back across the deck.

"Come on!" Antonio snapped, grabbing for the boy.

Squid extended his hand and something glittered in the corner of his eye. The cross was dangling below, precariously hanging from the ropes.

"Leave it!" Antonio barked.

Squid leaned over and reached for the cross. It shimmered back at him, the firelight dancing off its golden sheen.

He felt Antonio grab the back of his neck with one hand, lifting him. Squid stretched farther, managing to grasp the metal cold between the tips of his fingers.

"What are you doing?" Antonio gasped. "Damn it, boy! Are you trying to get yourself killed?"

The ship gave another jerk and Squid careened forward, holding tight to the cross. Antonio caught him, pulling him up towards the tallest part of the sinking ship.

The whale's shadow loomed over them, splitting through the water and crashing against the ship.

Squid saw Dougan's body go limp as it flew through the air, the aft quickly sinking beneath his feet.

"Follow me. We're going to jump," Antonio shouted.

Holding the boy in one hand and his harpoon in the other, Antonio leapt overboard.

The ocean swelled with the sinking ship, bubbling and rippling as the ship melted into the blackness below.

Squid bobbed on the surface, still clutching the cross. He watched the ship twirl in a slow circles, like some blue-grey ghost, far down beneath him. Broken pieces of the vessel littered the ocean around them, the gulls squawking angrily over their heads. Bodies floated by, the bright colors of the crew's clothing dotting the waves.

Dougan was still alive, floating on a piece of the mainmast. He looked calm now, as he stared up at the sky.

The giant's head lifted from the surface behind him. Captain Dougan turned to stare into its gaping mouth. The Dragon closed his eyes, letting the creaking jaws fall over him.

Squid gawked as the creature swam past, the twisted form of the captain red in its jaws.

"So ends the Dragon," Antonio muttered. "Just a man after all, not much of one at that."

The whale released the body, allowing it to sink to the bottom. Then it rolled, its head swerving to greet the two survivors.

Antonio swam over, placing himself in front of Squid.

The whale paused before him, still in the ocean, peering at the harpooner with its one good eye, creaking with its mouth of hanging teeth.

Antonio stared forward at the whale. The ocean grew silent and calm, the broken pieces of the ship slowly drifting away from one another atop the rolling waves. The birds stilled, hovering above them with wings outstretched.

Treading water, he raised his harpoon up. He held it up high, slowly lowering it into the sea, looking intently at the whale the whole time as he made his offering.

He swam calmly, slowly releasing the harpoon from his fingers and letting it sink before the whale's gaze.

Lazarus stilled, watching the heavy iron sink, his gaze growing misty. Squid thought the whale's remaining eye looked tired, mournful even, as it turned to stare back at Antonio.

The whale hovered for a long moment on the surface, breathing calmly, attention remaining fixed on the whaler and boy.

Then the mouth closed, a massive swell forming in the wake of the whale's turning.

"Go now," Antonio whispered reverently, watching the departing whale.

The beast made a low, creaking call and sank back into the sea. Its tail rose up straight before vanishing quickly into the blackness.

Squid looked around. His heart ached for the ancient creature. He felt hollow and more alone than he had ever felt before. Antonio swam over, and his heavy hand patted Squid on his head as if to wake him from his trance. He felt comforted by Tony's touch. It roused him as he concentrated again on treading water.

Nothing remained but debris and ocean birds, pecking at the floating dead. A syrupy, golden light coated the sky, the sea a vast, shimmering mass, rolling infinitely into the horizon.

Squid swam, the golden cross, a hollow thing, surprisingly light in his grip. "What now?" He asked.

A piece of the main deck was still afloat, bobbing ahead of

them. Antonio swam towards it and hooked his arms over it. Squid paddled and leapt on top of it.

Fins began appearing in the water, skimming along the surface, nudging at the dead.

"We best go now," Antonio said. "The sharks will feast well today."

Antonio pointed towards the green in the distance. "Home, Squid. We'll go home now. Just keep kicking until we reach the sands."

They kicked with their feet in the water for what seemed like hours, Squid despairing they would never feel the island beneath them. The blue fins followed, Antonio wrenching off a piece of the floating deck to swat one away.

The cross was slippery in Squid's palm; he worried about dropping it. The sun pierced low in his vision. And then he saw a line of black specks darting towards them.

Squid shielded his eyes with his hand to get a better view. Longboats! Azoreans from the village, perhaps a dozen.

Cabral's head was swaddled; he looked out at his friends through swollen eyes. The big African flashed a wide smile and waved.

Antonio howled, yelling for him at the top of his lungs.

"I rowed towards the smoke!" Cabral called out. "You were always more trouble than you were worth. Any ship with you aboard is surely doomed!"

Cabral grabbed Squid from out of the water, embracing him.

The whalers shook hands, Cabral quickly handing Antonio an oar, a mocking smile on his broad face. "No way I'm rowing today. You're always expecting me to do all the work."

"But how did you survive? I saw you fall," Squid blurted.

"Aye!" Cabral said. "A hard knock, but I lived."

They sat in the longboat for a long moment, the Azoreans nodding from their longboats in grim greeting.

"So, it's over," Squid muttered.

"Aye," Antonio said. "I think this business is done, an end to the voyage."

The Azoreans rowed in stunned silence towards the island, Squid and Antonio sitting hunched and exhausted in the rear of Cabral's boat. The oar Antonio had been handed sat uselessly across his lap. For the first time in his life, he was too spent to row.

"What is that?" Squid asked, seeing Cabral kick something underneath his seat.

Cabral raised an eyebrow. "You'll see."

They neared the beach with the sun hanging low in a purple twilight sky.

Figures stood amongst the black rocks, waiting. The women welcomed their men home, their long, black dresses and billowing hoods fluttering in the sea's salty breeze.

Squid's legs felt an aching stiffness as he leapt off the longboat, crunching against the sand.

Aldo was carried out from the forest, his chest crisscrossed with bandages. The big dog was with him, panting happily at Squid, its massive tongue trailing.

Squid ran up to the old priest, the dog leaping, lapping at his face.

More villagers began filing out of the forest, spreading along the beach. The old whaler from the cemetery was there, moving slowly through the palms. For a moment, Squid thought he could see his mother among them, a vision from out of the green.

The village still smoldered behind them. The wall was a broken heap, the church blackened by fire and smoke. The statue of the great angel still stood, staring out at the sea.

Squid kneeled, handing the priest his golden cross. The twilight caught its ruby center, making it sparkle.

Aldo's tear-filled eyes flew open, his ashen whiskers spreading into a smile.

Aldo took the cross, the people gathering around him, kneeling and crossing themselves before it. Aldo raised his shaking arms, blessing them before the roaring tide.

A big hand rested on Squid's shoulder. Antonio dragged him in for a heavy embrace, his voice booming with laughter. "This is a good place, boy. A good place to call home."

Everyone shook hands, kissed and hugged along the beach— all except Cabral, ever grim and silent. He was busy mounting a head atop a tall pole, the head of Scrab. It was open-mouthed and soaking, the molars gaping at one side.

Cabral had found the body of the old pirate, or what was left of it, floating amongst the waves. The sharks had taken most of what Lazarus had left behind.

Cabral faced the grisly head towards the sea, and with Squid and the villagers of Luz watching, proclaimed it should stay there. Hoisted up forever as a warning ... a warning to all villainous men who dared land on these shores.

A warm, salty breeze blew over the beach, a hawk soaring in the sun's fading light.

The big dog pranced over towards the ghoulish trophy, staring out at the Atlantic. He sniffed the air, looked up and barked at Scrab's head, as if pleased with it.

year of our lord

1832

NEPTUNE'S BONES

Grandfather was a big man, bigger than most of the men from these parts. He moved slowly and ponderously, old muscles quivering with every strain.

The boy wasn't sure why they were out here at all and he was already missing home. "Avô, how much farther?"

"We're close. Not much longer now, see …," said the old man, pointing towards the hilly green shores.

One of the big ships sailed past, American, cramped with the desperate and forlorn. They were filled with people from Old Europe, people fleeing famine and poverty, all fresh with hope for the new world. The stink from the ship wafted over to their boat. Grandfather grimaced, shaking his head.

The boy's stomach rumbled, his head aching. He had wacked it on the little boat's boom when they first sailed out from the old wreck of a dock, his grandfather chuckling as he cursed.

He closed his eyes, imagining his mother preparing the morning meal with her hair done up, his brothers and sisters running about the courtyard. They lived close to the twin lakes: one turquoise and one blue. The different colors of the adjoining lakes made them famous, and the small boy was proud of his home. The town was set amidst a valley, vast and lush.

"Too pretty for words, this land," his father would often say. The boy had never ventured off São Miguel's coast before and was more than a little nervous about this trip.

But Avô insisted, and no one ever said no to his Avô. Grandfather was ancient, six feet tall maybe, despite being hunched over. He had a ruddy beard, white and grizzled, always cropped neat and short. His skin was a collection of splotches and freckles, his face wrinkled with a thousand crevices. A long scar, pale and crooked, ran across his brow.

His eyes were hidden behind thick, downy eyebrows, which were ghostly grey.

The boy would often visit him. He was alone now in his little seaside cottage since Grandma died. The boy loved him, but this was no surprise, as it seemed everyone did.

They landed on the southernmost island of the Azores, on

Santa Maria's hot beach, the sun at their backs.

The boy's neck felt swollen and cracked from the heat, his arms aching with every pull. They dragged the boat ashore. Avô stared up at the cliff face.

"What are we looking for?" the boy asked.

"You'll know when we see it, Antonio," said Avô.

The old man closed his eyes, his nose flaring, sucking in the salty air. There was something strange about the smell here, something rotten and fleshy sweet.

"It was here …"

"What was?"

"They told me it was here … this beach … it has to be this one."

An old shack lay a few meters off. Two fishermen sat with their nets by the shore, fumbling with the little knots and hooks.

The old man raised a big hand, heavy with thick, strangling veins. "Stay here, see if you can pull the boat up a little farther … no telling how long we'll be."

The boy watched the old man talk with two rough islanders, their dark eyes looking up at Avô suspiciously.

The boat was heavy, the white sand rumbling beneath its hull as the boy heaved with all his might.

"There!" he groaned, wiping the sweat from his brow.

He turned towards his grandfather. Avô didn't always say much, but he could be quite charming when he wanted to be.

The two fishermen were laughing and smiling at him.

One of the fishermen pointed up past the cliffs. Avô nodded and strolled up beyond the white beach towards the cliff face.

"It's here. We have to climb."

The boy shrugged, following the old man up the rough path. Stone steps led the way, broken and crooked with creeping, thick vines crawling up out of them.

He tried not to look down, his stomach lurching as he stared at the distant waves.

Avô kept climbing, his big feet planting heavy on the shattered old steps.

They stopped to catch their breath at the top. Avô produced a crude pipe from his woolen coat.

The boy turned, watching the water glimmer as far as he could see. He wondered at everything beyond here, the big places—cities and countries so vast you could lose yourself in them completely. No one would know or care who you were. He felt tiny, insignificant. He looked about the island.

They were still in the green of the island, the tree growth and fauna quite familiar to him.

Avô placed a hand on his shoulder, blowing thick smoke rings into the hazy air with his pipe. "Pretty," he said, staring past him.

The boy nodded. "How much farther, now?"

"Not far at all," said Avô, tapping out the remainder of his tobacco and placing the pipe back into his pocket. "They dragged it up here … how, I don't know … half burying it in the clay."

"What?"

Grandfather grinned. "Neptune's bones."

The boy knew better than to keep asking, following the old man as he trudged through the bush.

They walked silently, the boy shuffling behind his grandfather's wide, stooping gait.

Avô froze ahead of him, peering out at a vast field of orange-red clay.

"Not much can grow here in the west," Avô muttered. "The settlements are mostly to the east, the island grows lush there, much like ours does."

Avô let out a long breath, pointing a thick, calloused finger at something rising up out of a field of red.

"What is that?" the boy gasped.

"Come," Avô said, his eyes distant.

The boy felt himself gasp at the sight of it. Something enormous had been planted in the ground yards ahead, made up of hard things, gleaming white and pearly in the sunlight. At first the boy thought they had been sculpted somehow, a cage of enormous ribs, pointing upwards from the clay. They were the bones of a giant creature.

A strange, flat skull rested on the ground, gigantic, the long jaw set precariously beside it. The teeth looked worn and worked down, the jaw bones splotched yellow and grey.

A set of vertebrae lay linked together on the ground—a crooked and bony path. The ribs were almost touching at the tips, rising high before him, tall and imposing.

As they walked up, the boy saw the bones were covered in small scar patterns and notches, one side of the ribs grown crooked with long gashes in its ivory. *Wounds of some sort,* thought the boy. Shafts of wood and sharp iron lay everywhere around it, like strange offerings.

Avô walked up to it, stroking the ancient bones with trembling hands. The old man reached into his shirt, pulling out the old medallion, worn with a gritty shine. The boy had never seen him without it, his Saint Michael's charm.

"What do you think those bones were from?" the boy exclaimed. "Did all that come from the same animal? Was it some monster? A sea monster? Or is it really Neptune?"

"No God, no monster … just a whale, a big, old whale."

The boy watched a tear roll down his grandfather's leathery face, trickling down his white whiskers.

The boy reached for his hand, clasping the old man's shaking fingers.

"They're just bones, Avô. Just bones."

Avô smiled, resting his arm over the boy's shoulder.

"I want to go home, Avô."

The old man nodded, removing the old medallion from his neck and handing it to him.

"Would you keep that for me?" his grandfather said, clasping the boy's fingers over the metal.

The boy grinned and nodded.

"Good, now we can go home."

The boy hugged him and the two trudged back across the clay field.

The sun was shining high over the islands. It was a fair day, golden and bright. Maybe the journey back would be easier.

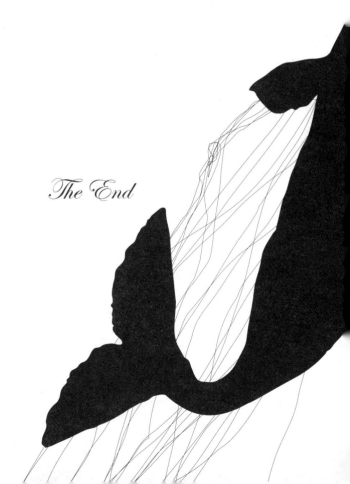

The End

ACKNOWLEDGMENTS

I spent most of my summers as a boy with my grandfather on the island of São Miguel. He was a house painter, did restoration work and was also a sometimes carpenter who did very well for himself. I followed him to work most days, finding any excuse to do anything other than work. It was in one of these worksites that I dug up a big whale's tooth. I remember him grinning at the sight of it, smiling with wonder at the strange thing. He assured me that I could keep it. He was a grand storyteller and was always making up tales. The high walls and towers that abound on the island became battlegrounds and overgrown gardens full of old magic in my grandfather's imagination. I owe him much, including the beginnings of this story. I will be forever grateful to him.

My wife was the first to read this book. Her love of the sea and all things nautical guided me straight and true. Without her there would be no books or inspiration to write. She is my strength and muse.

Many thanks to Lindsey Aubin, who helped give my many ramblings structure.

My buddy Vasko, for the general advice of "shut up and write the thing already."

Dimiter Savoff, for always believing in my work. Kallie George, who performs miracles with my writing and my editor Lara LeMoal, who gave life to these many pages. I also can't forget Heather Lohnes for helping me finish this book with real diligence and care for its story.

The following books were most helpful: *A History of World Whaling*, by Daniel Francis; *The Whale: In Search of the Giants of the Sea*, by Philip Hoare; *The Pirate Hunter: The True Story of Captain Kidd*, by Richard Zacks; *Moby Dick*, by Herman Melville.

I did a lot of listening to David Attenborough. His television documentary *The Blue Planet* was invaluable and I highly recommend it.

The whale's tooth my grandfather gave me was never far from me as I wrote this book. I suppose it is only right to thank that poor whale. God rest its great soul.

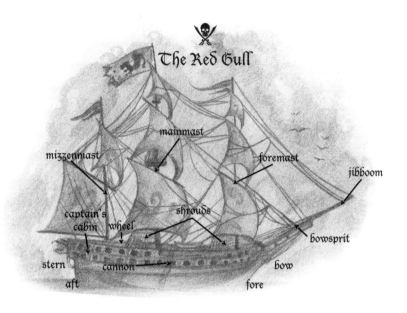

The Red Gull

mainmast
mizzenmast
foremast
jibboom
captain's cabin
wheel
shrouds
bowsprit
stern
cannon
bow
aft
fore

"Consider the subtleness of the sea; how its most dreaded creatures glide under water, unapparent for the most part, and treacherously hidden beneath the loveliest tints of azure. Consider also the devilish brilliance and beauty of many of its most remorseless tribes, as the dainty embellished shape of many species of sharks. Consider, once more, the universal cannibalism of the sea; all whose creatures prey upon each other, carrying on eternal war since the world began.

Consider all this; and then turn to the green, gentle, and most docile earth; consider them both, the sea and the land; and do you not find a strange analogy to something in yourself? For as this appalling ocean surrounds the verdant land, so in the soul of man there lies one insular Tahiti, full of peace and joy, but encompassed by all the horrors of the half-known life. God keep thee! Push not off from that isle, thou canst never return!"

— HERMAN MELVILLE, *MOBY DICK*

THE PREDATORS

BLUE SHARK

ORCA (KILLER WHALE)

RIGHT WHALE

GIANT SQUID

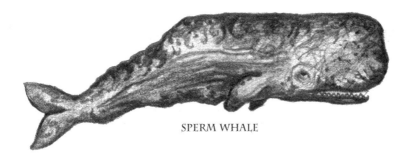

SPERM WHALE

Published in 2016 by Simply Read Books
www.simplyreadbooks.com

LIBRARY AND ARCHIVES CANADA CATALOGUING IN PUBLICATION

Moniz, Michael, author, illustrator
Whalemaster / written and illustrated by Michael Moniz.

ISBN 978-1-927018-79-8 (pbk.)
I. Title.
PS8626.O54W43 2015   jC813'.6   C2015-902464-1

We gratefully acknowledge for their financial support of our publishing program the Canada Council for the Arts, the BC Arts Council, and the Government of Canada through the Canada Book Fund (CBF).

Printed in Canada.

Book design by Michael Moniz
and Heather Lohnes.

10 9 8 7 6 5 4 3 2 1